T0129989

THE STORY OF 30

ANSLEY ANDERSEN

BALBOA.
PRESS
A DIVISION OF HAY HOUSE

Balboa Press books may be ordered through booksellers or by contacting:

Balboa Press
A Division of Hay House
1663 Liberty Drive
Bloomington, IN 47403
www.balboapress.com.au
1 (877) 407-4847

Because of the dynamic nature of the Internet, any web addresses or links contained in this book may have changed since publication and may no longer be valid. The views expressed in this work are solely those of the author and do not necessarily reflect the views of the publisher, and the publisher hereby disclaims any responsibility for them.

The author of this book does not dispense medical advice or prescribe the use of any technique as a form of treatment for physical, emotional, or medical problems without the advice of a physician, either directly or indirectly. The intent of the author is only to offer information of a general nature to help you in your quest for emotional and spiritual well-being. In the event you use any of the information in this book for yourself, which is your constitutional right, the author and the publisher assume no responsibility for your actions.

Any people depicted in stock imagery provided by Thinkstock are models, and such images are being used for illustrative purposes only. Certain stock imagery © Thinkstock.

Print information available on the last page.

ISBN: 978-1-5043-0199-2 (sc)
ISBN: 978-1-5043-0200-5 (e)

Balboa Press rev. date: 05/20/2016

CHARACTERS

Following is a fictitious story demonstrating the ugly faces of Human beings in our turmoil World. At the end of the story the author requests readers to judge and debate what is black and what is right. This is without any legal responsibilities from author under any circumstances.

CHAPTER 1

On this planet of Staton there is a family. This Ree family is a rich family where head of the family comes from another planet in the Universe. The head Relau is doing business of jewellery and has one wife and four concubines. They are a harmonious family. Fortunately, after Relau's death the family breaks down to every single pieces and Relau's decedents no longer follow Relau's teachings. That is to go to bed early and get up early in the morning. After Relau's death his granddaughter goes to sleep no earlier than 12-midnight.

However, Relau has a friend in Lung family. The old lady is only looking at your wealth no others. This old woman Lei has seven sons, five daughters and 26 grandchildren. One of the grandchildren Leather is getting married tonight and the whole family is enjoying the party.

When the party is finished Leather and his new married wife go back to Leather's home which is the home of the whole family at that time of the year. During the party many photographs are shot. In every photograph the bride always looks down at the floor. Other people think she is shy. But Leather's father looks very happy and is shot laughing in every photograph.

When the new couple arrives home Lei says to Leather's wife Terri at her back quietly, "You are a prostitute." In the first 15 years of life in this Lung family home Terri does all housework while Leather only sits there talking to his siblings or reading newspaper. Terri asks for his help but Leather only replies he can do nothing.

In the first 12 months of the new life Leather goes to work in daytime then sometimes goes home for dinner while most of the nights Leather is out with his friends gambling and dinner in a restaurant. Leather's father Laws is in bad mood every night when he comes back from his family office or family business. When Laws is home Lei tells Laws that Terri is not working properly. She uses too much gas when cooking food and too much water in washing the clothes. Meanwhile Laws's two daughters in order to make Lei happy simply to say similar comparisons.

At the end of 10 months Terri has a new born baby Tense. Laws comes back home sometimes shouts at Tense but sometimes gives money to this boy to buy sweets. Honestly, when Tense is grown up. He wishes to be an attorney but is obstructed by his father Leather who uses any dirty trick to stop Tense's legal study.

Leather always tells other people that Leather goes to swim early in the morning before goes to work. Leather explains when he was young. His body is very weak. It is why he goes to swim every morning for 10 years.

Fortunately, Leather's paternal uncle Less always wakes up early in the morning to exercise his body. He learned some skills while he was in a circus and now he still exercises with those acrobat techniques. Meanwhile Less's body is stronger and stronger. But look at Leather his body is weak. Whenever winter comes Leather is sure to catch a flu and cough with running noses. Leather swims for 10 years but has a fragile body. Why? At later life Leather goes to the beaches to swim with his friend. His friend swims from that beach to another beach. Leather's friend is able to swim such a long distance. While Leather goes back home with his wife and 5 kids as soon as possible.

When Tense is grown up and Laws is passed away. Tense talks to Terri and used to say that Tense wants to bring Leather to justice. Terri discloses to Tense that at early stage Leather's sisters tell Terri that they had gone to dinner with Leather just hours ago. Why they went? It is all because they pretended to be good sisters but indeed they hate Leather very much. It is all because when they were young they were treated as inhuman by Leather. Now it is their turn to revenge as their mother had died more than 10 years ago.

In the court room,

"Mr Leather, do you recall your office boy named Cha who eyes at your son Tense for at least 3 times during the period Tense is working in your company LL?"

"No, I have no idea!"

"Does anyone tell you regarding this matter?"

"No, utterly rubbish!"

"What's your opinion on Cha?"

"He is a good employee."

"He deserves a higher salary than your biological son Tense. Is that right, Mr Leather?"

"………………….."

"He is a good boy. Why at later date you command your brother Letton to insult Cha to let Letton's 2 sons to argue over Cha?"

"No such thing at all!"

"At your migration Cha says he has done all the things for you. From that time onward he will retreat and goes to another company to work and wishes you good luck. Is that right?"

"Yes, absolutely!"

"Does he still introduce girls to Tense?"

"I think so. What's wrong with it?"

"By your understanding any girls who Tense has chased that the girl is introduced by Cha?"

"I have no idea at all!"

"Isn't that Tense refuses to chase those girls as introduced by your followers?"

"I don't understand what you are talking about!"

"At that time do your followers show up to say or imply to Tense that the girls are introduced by them meanwhile Tense must obey them and to chase these girls?"

"I don't know!"

"Does Tense actually chase these girls?"

"…………………."

"Afterwards these people turn up in front of Tense and with your influence that tell Tense to chase the actress. Is that correct, Mr Leather?"

"I have no idea!"

"They first said they will stay behind as the affair is over. But later on these people re-appear to introduce girls to Tense and oblige Tense to follow. Is it correct, Mr Leather?"

"What are you talking about?"

"I am asking your conscience to tell you to disclose all the truths and valid facts to this court to evade your severe penalty and return to the right track, Mr Leather!"

"……………."

In the court room,

"Mr. Leather do you recall you do not help your wife in the housework but hanging around?"

"This is her duty to work in our house."

"What duties?"

"She is the daughter-in-law she has to work all her life time. It is nothing serious."

"Mr. Leather, you do not help her means you are correct?"

"Of course!"

"Do you remember at later life you wash the floor with your wife together at your residential home. But after one or two washings Tense replaces your position. Why?"

"Tense sees myself having neck pains and back bone disorder that is no good and I have brain cancer. So Tense tells me he does it with Terri."

"At that time you are a happy man, then?"

"It is said by Tense."

"At first you cut the grass. Later Tense replaces your position. Why is that?"

"He said he will do it and I sometimes go out and have no time to cut the grass."

"Sometimes go out. Go where?"

"To have some food or my younger son drives me to a beach."

"Did Tense go with both of you?"

"No, he didn't."

"Why?"

"…………"

"You just said you do not have time to cut the grass. Why you have no time? Is that no time to cheat?"

"Of course not."

"What then?"

"……………"

"What are you doing at home?"

"I wake up early in the morning to buy newspaper to read."

"Then?"

"I sometimes go to lunch with my friends or nephews and buy some food back home for dinner for the whole family."

"You are always busy on this?"

"Yes. I am not working now. What can I do, then?"

"You go out with your younger son Lance and only two of you. It means only two of you know what you were doing and what did you talk to each other. Am I correct?"

"We only gossip."

"Once you talk with Lance late at night in the sitting room. Suddenly Terri and Tense both walk in to the sofa sit down listen to your conversation. But finally you shout at them to go back to the bedroom. Am I correct?"

"……………."

"You always tell other people you went to swimming pool to swim even in winter for 10 years. You say anyone did not turn up would be fined $1. Am I correct?"

"Yes. Absolutely!"

"You catch a flu or a cold and cough every winter of the year. Why is that?"

"My body becomes weak."

"Weak! You have swum for 10 years. Then suddenly became so weak as not to resist the winter gusty wind but catch a flu. Can you explain why?"

"I have to work mornings till nights. It makes me weaker and weaker."

"No other reasons?"

"No. Definitely not!"

"Did you really swim for 10 years?"

"Yes, of course!"

"But it ends up with a fragile body always to see a doctor?"

"What's wrong with it?"

"There is nothing wrong. The question is did you actually go to swim or you went there just stood in the swimming pool to talk to other swimmers instead of swam?"

"No. Nonsense!"

"At later time you go to swim with Tense. You shout at Tense by saying he swims one lap and takes a break is of no use. Is it correct?"

"Yes, I do shout at him."

"Then Tense swims 20 or 30 laps in breast style. Right?"

"Absolutely!"

"What are you doing then?"

"…………….."

"You stand there to watch the girls. Right?"

"No, definitely not!"

"What are you doing ?"

"………………………….."

"Other swimmers in the pool are witnesses that you watch girls instead of swimming in the pool. Is that correct, Mr Leather?"

"…………………."

"When your elder son Tense recalls. One of your friends Mr. Chun says you go to night club to dance with the club girls. Is that correct?"

"Totally rubbish."

"Rubbish! What are your good conducts towards your wife then?"

"She marries me needs to do all housework and take care of my younger sisters and brothers. Otherwise what is the option to marry a girl?"

"Your wife that is Ms Terri once tells her son not your second son but your elder son that Terri works from mornings till nights. Also everyday your relatives no matter aunts or uncles go to your family house and say the same nasty thing to Terri in consistence with your grandmother Lei said. Do you know that?"

"Yes, I know some tiny details."

"Some tiny details. What details?"

"My sisters and siblings curse Terri in order not to let her has a comfortable life in our family."

"And then?"

"This is all I know."

"Really? Terri tells Tense that she is so angry that she cries in the bedroom. All her grievances are told to neuropsychologist Dr Dung. And Dr Dung is a relative of your good friend Dung naked named 'Barber'. Is that correct?"

"I only know the truth from that time."

"Your sisters Lin and Lie both have a chance to urge you to move away from the family house but you prefer to stay. Is it correct?"

"I think so."

"Tense learns from Terri at that time Terri was happy to move out of the big house and stay in tiny rooms or in nasty suburbs together with you. Do you recall this?"

"Yes, this is truth."

"Then why do you not move, Mr. Leather?"

"If we moved out I could not find a job simply because I do not have much school study when I was young."

"At that period of time there are many evening school teaching people some work skills and some literacy. Why do you not attend these evening schools and work on day time?"

"Well, I have problems."

"What problems?"

"It is the duty of sons to follow their father's way of conduct and to receive father's business as a good child in the family."

"Oh! I see. You stay."

"Yes."

"Did you tell your brother Leson on this issue?"

"Yes, I did."

"What did you say?"

"I told him I will still talk to my father but not two of them."

"Did you do that?"

"Yes, I did."

"Why did you still talk to your sisters or at least only on some occasions. While you always talk with their sons and daughters?"

"They are my relatives."

"They were rich?"

"Yes, at that time."

"Afterwards what happened?"

"I did not talk to them."

"At that time your paternal uncle Mr. Choy was in partnership with you on business. Meanwhile the company was having a huge profit. Am I correct?"

"Yes."

"At that time you quarrelled with the two sisters?"

"Yes."

"Why did you wait to such a long time after the incident?"

"I was not so angry yet."

"After your father's death all family members discussed how to distribute the business and money. Is it true?"

"Yes. Absolutely."

"But you quarrelled with Lie accusing her to harm your wife and yourself. Did it really happen at that time?"

"Yes."

"Why you lose mood in a sudden instant and becomes surprisingly friendly in a short time afterward?"

"I use to tolerate."

"Oh! You always tolerate."

"Yeah!"

"Later on why you see Tense eats a lot of food when he is working in your company LL that every time you see this, you lose your mood?"

"I have never ever seen anybody to eat so much."

"Really?"

"Definitely!"

"Isn't that Tense starts to eat a lot from the second he was born?"

"……………"

"Before you migrated overseas you told Terri you are going to harmonise with these two sisters. Am I correct?"

"Yes, that is right."

"Why did you say that?"

"They are my blooded sisters. We are from the same parents."

"Only these?"

"Of course. What's wrong?"

"At that time you forgot all your hatred to your sisters?"

"We are in the same family."

"You are good brothers and sisters?"

"Certainly."

"Is it not at that time you were having a power struggle with your second younger brother Little to strive for commandership in the family?"

"No, absolutely not."

"Return to your childhood education. Why did you go to work in the family office as a bookkeeper?"

"I was told by Less to work there."

"And then?"

"And then I work there for 20 years."

"Later on your grievances on this issue is that you were called to work and instead you did not have the chance to go to school. Is that correct?"

"Yes, I was told to work at a young age and missed the opportunity to study while I was young."

"Later on you grumble on this topic and regret to work to miss school. Is that correct, Mr Leather?"

"I am very annoyed!"

"As stated why you listened to Less to work instead of to study?"

"I was told and have no options!"

"If you were still continuing to study were you happy on that?"

"Of course, I would learn more."

"Mr Leather, is it true that you did not revise your lessons after school instead go out to play or do something else and not reading the books or textbooks?"

"....................."

"If you were continuing to study. Would you guarantee you would get a good mark and be promoted every year?"

"............................."

"Now, back to Tense and Terri,

"When your son is born not the second son. When he is born Terri needs to go to the theatre for labour. At that time the cost is $1,000. But you cannot afford to pay this amount. Why?"

"It is the father's obligation to pay hospital fees for his grandchildren."

"At that time your income is $600 a month. After marriage you go out to dinner most of the week nights with either your friends or the business friends. Is it correct?"

"Yes, it is."

"You are living in your family house. You do not need to worry the rental payment nor shopping money. After 10 months you cannot afford to pay $1,000. Is this correct?"

"As I mentioned it is the duty of a father to look after their children and grandchildren."

"When you are having this baby and it is almost time for labour. But your father goes overseas to Kote and not care of your new born baby is coming to this world. After the new baby has come to this world your grandmother also goes to Kote to tell any person she knows that you cannot afford to pay the hospital fee but rely on your father. Am I right?"

"………………. It should be paid by my father……………."

"After your marriage you do not allow Terri to go out even with her own sisters. Why?"

"They are no good."

"Where are the no goods?"

"One of them is arrogant because of her wealthy husband. The other is poor always come to get old clothes or old furniture to bring back to her home and all of them used to gossip this and that exactly like those women have nothing to do but saying others' affairs."

"The wealthy sister Tele always urges Terri to go out not secluded in the house. Is she wrong?"

"Women are to be closed in their bedrooms and never go out."

"This is feudalism, is this not?"

"I was taught on this at school."

"You always tell your friends and especially your elder son Tense that your father is old-fashioned-minded old man. He always listens and trusts all other people on what they have said. Now you are doing the same. Am I correct?"

"My father is old-fashioned. This is known by all our relatives and he does behave in this manner without any considerations or to clarify any of people's sayings and he is happy on this. It is certain that he does not care what other people think."

"Your father is old-fashioned-minded. What is your idea? Old-fashioned or modern?"

"I am working for most of my life. I encounter many people or different types of people. I understand old-fashioned is not a good thing to follow."

"That means you are not old-fashioned?"

"Of course not."

"Once Tense was having dinner with your father Laws together with your sister Las. Suddenly Tense screamed that the other sister Lan is a bad woman. Las immediately stopped Tense. Do you know this matter?"

"No, I do not."

"After 3 or 4 weeks Tense goes to the office. As soon as Tense steps inside the office premise Laws rushes forward to utter something at Tense' ear."

"Do you know this?"

"No."

"At that time Tense is concentrating on other people's conversation. Afterwards while Tense is walking to the sofa closed to the wall of your family office. Tense suddenly recalled what Laws has just said and Tense deduces Laws is not feudalism. Do you know this?"

"No."

"Now I have just told you this. What is your response?"

"Tense is crazy."

"Crazy. Why crazy?"

"Tense always thinks of ugly things which are non-sense and without logic."

"Really?"

"Of course!"

"When did it start?"

"Around 11 or 12 years old."

"At that time Tense watched the TV series describing a famous lawyer always finds out who is the murderer. Is that around that period of time?"

"I can't remember."

"When you know and realise Tense is working towards a lawyer. Then you start to say Tense's ideas are all non-sense. Is it not?"

"No."

"If Tense becomes a lawyer. Then he understands the legal system. Also you understand Tense will not commit any crime but not the other family members. It is this reason you obstruct Tense to study Law course in University. Am I correct?"

"Why I did that?"

"Simply because your family members all commit crimes as what I have said."

"Are you crazy?"

"At your later life you are tied to a court case. At that time period it is found out your paternal uncle Less used the company money to invest on his own business. Is it correct?"

"Yes, he did it."

"Is it a crime?"

"Of course it is!"

"You are happy to point out this matter in the court room to help your cousin to sue Less?"

"He actually did it!"

"Is it a crime?"

"………………………….."

"On your behalf when you were working in your family office. There is a leger the company keeps and never report to Tax Office for company tax at every financial year. Is that correct?"

"It is Less's ugly idea."

"You do not object?"

"What can I do? I am under him in the company. I have to listen to him."

"Listen to him. Really a good boy."

"If I do not listen to Less. My father is not happy."

"Your father is not happy. Really?"

"He is old-fashioned!"

"You are Laws's son. You cannot oppose Less?"

"Of course I can't!"

"The other brother of yours always quarrel with Laws' younger sister named Leve about what method to do business. To make your family business more prosperous.

He quarrelled with Leve meanwhile you dare not quarrel with Less?"

"I am a good boy."

"Do you love your wife Terri?"

"Of course I do."

"You do! Why Terri suffers so much hardships but you tell Terri you will return to harmony with your sisters and brothers even they hurt and damaged Terri's early married life?"

"They are my siblings. Simple as that!"

"How about I ask you this question. You love your wife or you love your sisters and brothers?"

"They are my blooded family members."

"That means Terri does not deserved to be loved and should suffer so many burdens and without any single resentment?"

"She has to do all the housework."

"This is the way you love Terri?"

"Many people praise me as a good husband!"

"Good husband! Whenever there are people round there. You speak to Terri in a soft voice. While there is no one in vicinity you shout at Terri. Am I correct?"

"You are wrong!"

"Where am I wrong?"

"..."

"While Tense is working in your own company LL. The office boy eyes at Tense for 3 or 4 times and Tense loses his mood to quarrel with you. Is that true?"

"At that time I really could not work out the reason why he was so angry and suddenly burst into quarrel."

"You have no idea?"

"Of course not!"

"After your migration your brother goes back to home town with his whole family. Isn't that Little goes to LL to visit your business partner?"

"He told me this."

"In the meantime the office boy Cha is always showing off to Little's 2 sons. Am I correct?"

"I have no idea!"

"One morning before Little returns to homeland. Little brings the 2 sons to visit you. Is it correct?"

"May be!"

"At that time his 2 little sons talk to Tense about Cha. Tense replies 'only good at small unimportant things is useless'. Immediately, the 2 boys go out to inform their father and they leave. Am I correct?"

"I think so."

"Is it true that you told Little to go up to LL and finds any single chance to humiliate Cha?"

"Non-sense!"

"Then why Little visits you on that morning?"

"We are blooded brothers."

"Oh! What a good excuse! Blooded brothers."

"Of course we are!"

"You did not send Little to LL. While you do not hate the employee even he cheated you as he pretends to be a good boy and worker?"

"I have no idea!"

"He cheated you successfully. It means he is a better liar than yourself. He cheats you also mean you are not experienced enough to find out between truth and void. That means you have no face. Is it correct?"

"I do not hate Cha!"

"Really?"

"Of course!"

"That means even Cha eyes your son you are not going to fire him?"

"Tense is useless."

"Useless? I see. How about Cha? He is skilful?"

"Everyone knows!"

"You won't sack Cha?"

"Why should I?"

"He insults your biological son and you still let him stay in LL?"

"What's wrong with it?"

"It means you are a good man and even Cha cheated you but you again want him good. Is this what you are thinking of?"

"I don't want to hate anyone!"

"Why then?"

"I learn from Mrs Great to be a friend with anybody."

"Oh! I see. But why do you always curse your brothers-in-law? That is Terri's brothers."

"They are naughty boys."

"Cha is a good boy?"

"………………"

"Jury, just having heard what I have cross-examined Mr Leather. Do all jurors believe in what he has just given the answers regarding my questions just asked? Did he reply honestly? Or we say he is a big liar? Or he is a man with crocodile face and a heart of snake? I want to ask jury can we believe in such a man or we need to sentence this man as precedent to warn forthcoming people who want to commit the same crime as a hypocrite?"

Why Leather is saying all these lies simply he wants to show his gentleman-ship and conceals his hypocrisy. Why Leather stays in the family house is to show his good to Laws and final target is Laws's fortunes after Laws's death. It can be shown by one incident. Laws's daughter Lie urges Laws to purchase an organ to her. At that time Laws is under financial constrictions ban by his two brothers in the family business. It means Laws has to spend on a limited sum of money every month. Lie insists on the purchase. Finally, the organ is bought. Lie shows to Laws only several times to play this organ to teach the young children such as Lance how to play. Then nothing happens. Lie does not go to find a teacher to teach her nor put an ad on newspaper to call children to come forward as her organ students. The organ stays in the family house until it is sold when Lie moves overseas and the money is in Lie's own pocket.

Leather pretends to be a good son in front of Laws. But Laws has an idea. A horrible idea. It is to follow Leather to see where he goes to find out what Leather is doing. Maybe whenever Leather is talking with friends over the phone in the office to arrange dinner party on that night or some other nights. After Leather has left the office. Laws catches a bus, a cab or a tram to that restaurant and goes inside to see what is going on. Laws may hear Leather is gossiping with the club girls same as talking to sweet heart. Something like this. Laws finds out what Leather has done. It is why Laws hates Leather so much.

Again Leather always tells people after the first conversation with any one. Leather is sure to realise that person's characters. Is it true? Why? What Leather is saying in the conversation is all about his family's big businesses and owns commercial buildings. By saying all these if the person also praises Leather then that person is sure to be a good person. Otherwise that person is a bad creature or monster. This is the difference between good and bad people! Can anyone understand other person's characters after the first initial conversation? Tell me why!

Returning to Laws as Laws sees his offspring all aim at his fortune. At later life Laws is cursed by his own brothers something like to settle down on who owns what properties in the family or anyone is assigned to a certain family property from then on and that's it. No bothers in the future. Laws sees all these on his own feelings in a pitiful situation and regrets to let his brothers to join his business as partners. He hates his offspring lust for money, power, influences and reputations. But at that time what can Laws does? All are bad! May be the only hope is on Tense. But Tense by seeing these uncles and aunts at his later life. Tense refuses to help without regret nor sorry. There is no debt to that family from Tense. Regarding to Laws Tense has paid his debt by doing many things to help the family and his uncles and aunts. One more thing is that family owes a debt to Terri. Does Tense have to pay his debt or go to revenge? Tell me! The family is also owing a debt or debts to Tense, honestly.

Laws is so upset that he decides not to leave his Last Will that let the offspring to fight for his fortunes and teased by every single person who knows them. But indeed this doesn't help. The bad guys do bad things as they did before up to their last minute. The sons even take his daughters' marriages as business transactions. They urge the daughters to know wealthy sons wherever their mother and daughters go out to attract rich sons and their daughters to become friends with the rich boy. And then.......! This is good business, isn't it? Tell me!

As they do come from rich family they all show off. They do it days after days, weeks after weeks and years after years. All show off and find every single chance to grab power, reputation, influence and money especially after the collapse of the family business. At that time Leather tries to look for the help of Terri's brother Tom a billionaire. But Tom refuses. From then on both people never talk to each other not even coming face to face on the streets.

Leather's trick is not to let people know he is hypocrite and does nasty things. Whenever Leather does bad things either at that instance there is no relatives nor friends around in the premises and to do it secretly. Or after he has done nasty things he never ever tells other people. When he curses other people. At that time the person to be cursed is not present or the one listening to his curse does not know the whole details. Once Leather curses a friend Dr O by saying he did not repay his 30-thousand-dollar loan to Leather. But Tense finds out the time Dr O paid his debt, it happens twice, Tense is called by Leather to cross the harbour to apply certification for imported goods in Customs Office. When these happened Tense saw twice Dr O took back the loan docket as soon as Tense opened the company door on his return to Leather's company. Tense saw that Dr O had repaid the loan. Tense does not utter a single word when Leather is accusing Dr O for the loan. Why Leather accuses Dr O? simply at that time Leather meets so many setbacks and has no way to express his annoyances. Simple as that!

At that time everyone is saying Leather is going to give his business to Tense. Everyone is saying this. But Leather never ever tells Tense face to face on this matter. Simply Leather is giving the business to his second son Lance. God! Tense is happy on this when he finds out in later life. Tense owes no debt to this family! On the contrary the family owes many debts to Tense as Tense helped them a lot of times whenever they were in troubles. God!

When Tense grows older maybe at that time is 6 or 8 years old Tense heard people saying Tense needs special care immediately after he was born in the hospital. This information is later affirmed by Terri by telling Tense face to face.

When Terri is having the baby Tense. Leather buys some good food back home for the whole family especially for Terri to eat. While Leather is cooking the food his grandmother Lei says, "Are you preparing big meals to an Emperor?" After this Leather tells Terri grandmother Lei is not happy and stops buying more nutritious food for dinner. It is why Tense is under special care.

Before marriage Leather leaks a news to Terri by some other people. Saying Leather is very frightened of his father Laws. This is a pretext to let Leather to listen to Laws all the time. Leather loves money and reputation. No matter who cheats Leather. Leather is certain to revenge when Leather has got such ability and a chance.

Leather stays in family office simply he is the boss even deputy manager. But Leather still has power and reputation. By these all Leather's siblings have to listen to Leather. Leather said 'one' others dare not say 'two'. When Leather is in trouble. Leather will do anything you told him. But not to defamed his reputation. He is still a gentleman not a hypocrite at any time of his life.

When Leather is in cash flow troubles. Leather borrows money from his two brothers-in-law. Both charge Leather interest. Why? Their wife tells them all nasty thing Leather had done to them when they were young. Why Leather borrows money? Leather thinks that he is going to receive Laws' property and money. Then the brothers-in-law have to follow Leather. When Leather is in trouble. They definitely come over to help and always follow Leather. Tricky, isn't it?

Why Terri always looks at the floor in wedding party. Terri tells Tense that Terri right from the onset she does not love Leather. When Leather tells Terri to prepare for the wedding ceremony. Terri tells her parents she does not want to marry Leather. But Leather blackmails Terri and tells Terri's parents all necessary preparations are already done. Terri has no choice and is forced to get ready for the party.

Terri is very upset and her father suggests to bring Terri to flee away. This idea is later called off because Terri's mother believes in Leather's lies and the persuasion of Relau. Then tells Terri she will have a good life after marriage. Under these circumstances Terri has no options but marry. It is why Terri always looks at the ground. Why Leather does everything to let the wedding to go on smoothly. It may be to show to Laws he is matured and going to marry. By this it means Leather has told Laws that Terri is ready for the marriage. But suddenly Terri refuses to attend the wedding ceremony. It takes Leather in a very difficult and embarrassed position. Leather has no excuses to lie to Laws on what's going on. Thus, Leather needs to oblige Terri to say 'Yes'. Simply no other options!

CHAPTER 2

Tense grows older from infancy then Tense goes to kindergarten. Terri tells Tense some time later in their lives that Terri tells Tense to pour some water to drink. Tense immediately does it without taking off his school bag.

The first elementary school Tense attends is Silver Rocks Elementary and High School. In the first year Tense attends classes and goes back home. Day after day and week after week. No difference all over the year.

At this time there are 2 classes on the same level of school building. The class where Tense is studying which the classmates go to fight another class student with plastic rulers. Tense knows nothing but to follow. At every recess Tense follows students to fight. It ends up with broken rulers and Leather has to buy new rulers to Tense every now and then. After a while the fighting suddenly stops. But Tense knows nothing. Still waiting to fight at recess time. Tense waits and waits. On one day when Tense asks a classmate and he tells Tense the fighting has ceased for a while.

At this period Tense needs many rulers and once Leather asks him why using so many rulers. Tense cannot give an answer. Then Leather says are the rulers not strong enough and Tense immediately says yes.

At this time Tense learns from the aunts to smoke. Tense even buys a pack of cigarettes put inside the school bag. One night when the family are in the bedroom Lance suddenly takes out the cigarettes to ask Leather what it is? Tense immediately grabs back the pack to put it back inside the school bag. After this incident Tense throws away the cigarettes and not to smoke for a while.

After a few years Tense and Lance go to family house and see the aunts and uncles all gambling on the races. After a couple of times on seeing this Tense goes down to street to buy cigarettes and a booklet of the racing tips. Tense pretends in the bathroom and tells Lance to tell Tense which animal comes first. At that time Tense has no money but only circles the one Tense thinks fit or the name is good to be honest. Tense does all these inside the bathroom. After second thought Tense realises it is no help. Simply Tense does not bet with money and knows nothing and is always losing. Then stops and goes back to sitting room to watch television.

In the second year of elementary school there is a classmate always asks Tense something about his privacy. After a while Tense realises what he told the boy is seeming to say that Tense is a wealthy boy. Then Tense tries to stop. But the boy urges Tense to go to top floor of school building to gamble at every recess time. This lasts for 4 or 8 weeks. Tense thinks it is not fit but cannot say no. Tense suddenly has an idea. There may be someone tells the class-mistress on this matter. After a few days this really happens. The class-mistress tells Tense to stop. Tense happily says yes and no more gambling.

In saying gambling Leather and his siblings all interested in it. Leather gambles, drinks wine and goes to night club. While his brother goes to gamble till dawn. His brother even smokes same as his father Laws. Meanwhile Tense's aunt does not go to work after high school. She stays home and asks for money from her father Laws. Why she does not work? She always wants to work in a relative's office or the company boss is a friend of hers or belongs to her family members. By doing this the aunt is on top of other employees and these employees have to listen to the aunt and follow her. This means she is the boss besides the real boss. She has privileges.

It is why after Laws's death this aunt has not a single cent. Her sister helps her to ease money problems. At later life this aunt repays the debt by revenges to her sister's son and daughter. Now she begs the brother to support her to study in University somewhere else. But finally she succeeds and finishes the study. The brother who supports this aunt is best known to betray brothers and sisters to grab most of Laws's fortunes. She begs him. He betrays the siblings and she begs him!

After the study this aunt Loose goes back home. She immediately starts her revenge. Leather has no influence and no money in the meantime. Loose tries every single chance to insult Leather and says nasty words to anybody who knows Leather to defame Leather. Loose does not do this when Leather was once in power. Now she does!

Loose's younger sister always shows off which sometimes makes Loose in a difficult situation. But that sister 's husband has money. Loose does not retaliate on this sister and focus on Leather. Loose even tries hard to destroy Tense while Tense was in hospital. She tries any chance to make Tense's illness to return to an even worse position than before. But she fails every time. Why she does it? All these Loose never ever discloses a tiny single word to her husband. Otherwise her husband is not happy. Simply she knows her husband does not love her. Her husband has no options that finally marries Loose before their marriage takes place.

Loose is a snake. All the siblings are snakes. All family members are snakes. It is to wait and see when and how Fairy to manipulate the penalty verdict!

Once Tense is sick during childhood. Tense remembers the servant is not good to Terri. In an afternoon Tense is going to see a doctor with his parents. Tense vomits on the floor. At that time Tense thinks the floor will not be cleaned. Unfortunately, it is cleaned when they come back home. Tense does not know why?

When Tense is studying elementary school. At that time Tense is around 5 years old. His father Leather worries about Tense's safety. Leather asks the younger sister Lin to bring Tense back home after school. Lin always quarrels with Leather and refuses to do it. Tense then comes back home by himself. A few days later it is Sunday afternoon the whole family is having lunch eating bread and peanut butter. Lin says to Tense, "Tense, you do not eat the hard stuff of the bread. Same as me!"

From the born of Tense he is the favourite grandson of Laws, Leather's father. During this period that is before

Laws's death everyone is good and kind to Tense. Their pretext is Tense is a good boy and works hard in his study. Those people include Leather.

At the time when Leather is down and poor after his father's death. Leather has no money, no reputation and no influence. Even the cleaners of the office building curse Leather that 'You have no power now. You can't fire us. It is the time you are fired.'

Simply may be Leather ordered the cleaners to wash toilets and washing basins in a straight not lenient way. That is to clean them in perfect cleanliness. Not a single dirt. He is in power and the boss at that time. Otherwise you are fired! Later on Leather revenges by saying this event in front of Tense when Tense is having super natural feelings. Is Leather a gentleman or hypocrite? Or a means?

During this time there is no clue to work out how Leather knows a man Mr. Fan. At that time this man is rich. Leather always invites him to lunch and most of the times together with Tense. At lunch it is Leather does the talking and Mr Fan never ever utters a single word. Then after 3 years Leather is having a partnership with his paternal uncle Mr Choy. Most of the time when Leather is free and no need to lunch with clients. Leather calls Mr Fan to come over to lunch. Mr Fan immediately comes over. During these occasions to lunch with them if Tense is also at the scene. Tense only eats and no talk.

After a period of time especially when Tense is working in Leather's partnership company PL Company. Every time Mr Fan comes over Tense is in bad mood. No one knows why includes Tense at that time. A few years later Mr Fan's business is in trouble. He borrows money from Less controlled family business company. Afterwards Tense is working in Leather's own company LL Company. Mr Fan tries every single event to crush Tense.

The first time the office boy eyes at Tense. Then Cha is on leave to have a simple surgery. The very first day Fan comes to lunch together. Fan says something to let Tense to follow which the phrase is first spoken by Cha. It is to harm Tense by saying that Tense has to follow others without sovereignty. Not able to be independent and must follow other people. By this Fan can tell this fact to his friends or his wife to tease Tense having a good face but no independence. This Fan can express his anger to Tense and already retaliate to counteract to Tense's good facial expression which attracts many girls. Tense does not follow and Fan immediately stops talking.

After 2 or 3 years when Tense is gradually having super-natural feelings. Fan turns to a friendly face to say good words about Tense but only on the surface or pretends to be good. Fan wants to migrate to overseas but his business is in a mess and he borrows much money from Less's controlled company. Fan has no option but to please Tense for his super-natural feelings which may be an aid to his migration.

After successful migration Fan deserted Leather and Tense. He always goes to Leather's brother Little's home as visitor with Fan's wife to have dinner together. It is because Leather secretly signed a contract or agreement to allow Little to control all Leather's property and cash after Leather's death. Fan still wants to be on the upper-hand position such that not to beg Tense. When Fan is in trouble Fan asks Little to tell Tense to do this to do that. This is why Fan goes to Little's home right after Fan's migration.

One more incident Fan always says whenever a young person is going to be the manager of a firm. Fan curses the young has no experiments and no knowledge to manage the company. When Fan's offspring are all grown up. They become managers at once. Fan is saying on the pretext that Fan is happy to let them to do it simply Fan is old and wants to retire. Look at this!

Another evidence is Fan at first always says he goes to primary school when he is a boy. His grandfather always persuades him that Fan comes from a rich family the government is not going to let him has a chance to learn in a school. Fan insists to study. Finally, Fan studied for a few years then goes to business and earn profits and looks down upon Leather.

This matter Fan used to tell other people implying he is a good boy wants to learn. Later on because Tense always explains the reasons that entangled in puzzles. Fan is afraid that Tense deduces Fan loves money and this is the only reason why Fan studied. Then goes to do business to become a millionaire. Fan stops saying this matter from then on. Never ever utter a single word anymore! For ever!

A few years later once Leather calls from overseas to tell Tense to phone to Fan to bring some tablets to Leather when he goes to Leather's place to meet Leather on the following day. Fan first tells Tense to bring the tablets to Little's home because on that night Fan and Little are having dinner together. Tense does not drive a car. Can Tense go there? Tense hangs up.

Later Leather calls again to tell Tense to call Fan again. Tense does it. Fan's wife tells Tense that Fan has already gone out to look for which streets to go through in order to reach Tense's house because he does not know how to get to Tense's place. Fan does not speak the local language. Can he find and ask people? Tense lives on the same street as his relative Letton's home. Fan always goes to visit Letton but now he does not know how to go to Tense's place? It is a joke or a movie?

At 6:30pm Tense is almost finishing his dinner. Someone rings the door- bell. It is Fan. As soon as Tense opens the door Fan tells Tense at once that Fan does not know the way to drive to Tense's house and asks Little to direct Fan to come. Then immediately Fan walks away from the front door not to talk to Tense. Hoping Tense to greet Fan in a friendly way and say something good that other people listen to this conversation will assume Tense is a mean person. Tense does not let Fan to come inside the house.

Now it is Little's turn. Little immediately walks into the house and sees Tense is having dinner. Little seizes the telephone handset to ring to his wife saying to go out to dinner afterwards. It is because Leather wants to control Tense thus, Leather does not give money to Tense. By this Little is happy to see Tense to beg him to bring Tense to dinner. Leather always accuses Less uses economic policy to control other relatives. Leather does the same. Is he not?

On Tense's part he is very happy. It is because after Leather's death Tense together with Terri are able to desert the Lung family without owing the family a single coin or debt.

After a short while Little is having a fatal illness and is in deep trouble. Fan rings to Leather to chat over the phone for several times. Once Fan asks Leather where is he going to in the afternoon. Leather tells him Leather is going to casino. Fan says he will go there too and they can both talk whenever there is a chance. By doing this Fan has an old friend to rely on.

No matter what Fan is doing. He is refusing to talk to Tense or to beg Tense. Whenever Fan is in trouble and needs help. Fan's usual trick is to tell Leather the details and then let Leather to disclose to Tense in a conversation with any other person. Then it will induce Tense to want Fan to go over the burden and no more turmoil. As Leather is having a fatal disease thus, Fan goes to Little. Now Little is also having problems then Fan goes to Letton. On second thought it is better to retain a medium level contact with Leather in case some unexpected things happen. Hence, Fan tries to resume contact with Leather. Or Fan just only desert Leather for good simply Leather humiliate Fan lots of times before Fan's migration.

Again after a few years Fan is in trouble with the police and calls Leather. After the phone conversation Leather is having lunch. Tense asks what is going on? Leather first in black face but immediately changes to a worry face. Then nods his head. Tense tells Leather, "If it is true. I still have no plan to help!" Leather has nowhere to go and remains silence. What Fan has done is criminal offences. If you were Tense. Are you going to give Fan a hand? Tell me!

At that time Leather is very sick. Fan immediately visits Letton as many times as possible. Fan hates Tense so much that Fan is definitely not to beg Tense as stated above. If Fan has got any trouble Fan only asks Tense's relatives such as uncles and aunts to tell Tense. After Leather's death once Fan meets a man who used to talk to Leather when they were in casino. Fan promised the man to call Tense to give the man, a master, his telephone number to Tense. Actually Fan calls Letton to ask Letton to call Tense.

Tense deduces that after Letton has called and Tense calls to Fan. Fan will say he is so frightened that he has no courage to call Tense. It is because Fan thinks Tense is angry with Fan. From then on Tense will become good friends with Fan. Then whenever Fan has trouble especially commits a crime. Fan will pretend to be sorry and gives Tense a pitiful appearance to let Tense to try methods to protect Fan. Finally, Tense does not call Fan to not to involve in any turmoil.

Another point is when Tense does not call the master. Fan can say Tense looks down on the master and does not ring. At that time Fan can say anything he can to defame Tense in order to express Fan's anger onto Tense as Fan is facing many problems after migration. On a day Tense catches a bus to go out. On the bus Tense is very fatigue and closes his eyes. Then gets off. Actually the master and his wife catch the same bus. Tense gets off first and does not realise their existences. But Tense walks a few steps there is shower and Tense stands under a building. Now Tense sees the master and explain all the truths to them. From then on Tense sends cards to the master for 3 or 5 years and stops. As Tense is going to learn kick boxing and is moving away to another suburb.

Fan hates Tense too. Fan tries every single chance to destroy Tense. Only starting from when Tense has some supernatural feelings that Fan stops his cruelties and pretends to be a good friend of Tense. As usual every time after Tense's annoyance is over all these people still come out and still stay with friends with Tense. At that time Tense does not understand why. Finally, it is found out these people pretend to be good and try every opportunity to destroy Tense. Look at the office boy Cha. He and his brothers and sisters are planning to kill Tense whenever there is a chance. When Tense is learning kick boxing. Cha pretends to exercise in the office in the morning. This leads Tense to teach Cha what Tense has learned from master. Then Cha and his siblings will work out a technique to crush the attacks from Tense. Then kills Tense and saying Tense falls over by himself. Simple as this!

As Fan has to beg Tense to help Fan while at that time Fan is in financial troubles. Fan has no choice but to say something good to Tense to grab Tense's confidence on Fan then gradually controls Tense to work for Fan. Fan is also a hypocrite. Same as Leather. Is he not?

Fan even tells other people that his father-in-law once lived with Fan for 2 or 3 weeks. Fan goes out for dinner with his sons and daughter but his father-in-law refuses to go. During that period his father-in-law never utter any bad comments about Fan. It means Fan is a good man. If he is a good man. Why Fan was eager to go to study in primary school while Fan's grand-father used to tell him the government would not allow Fan to go to school? But Fan insisted. When Fan knows how to write and read Fan goes to business and became a rich man. Only years later he lost money on another business that caused him to go broke.

In the court room.

"Mr. Leather are you able to explain why you treat Tense better than your second son Lance?"

"It is because Tense has a better academic result."

"How about Lance's academic results?"

"He scores low marks."

"Low marks. That means you are not happy?"

"Yes, I am not."

"Why do you give 4 houses to Lance to receive rental income but Tense has only one house. And you say to Tense that the rental income is for his livelihood."

"Because he is a neuro-patient."

"Then you do not treat him kind?"

"He always loses his mood whenever I shout at him."

"Why do you shout at him?"

"I cannot understand why Tense eats so much. I never ever see a person eats a lot of food."

"Really?"

"When Terri is pregnant she eats lots of food every meal every day. You do not realise, do you?"

"Well! Tense needs to change his habit to eat less."

"He needs to eat less!"

"Certainly."

"Then why do you always go out for dinner in restaurants?"

"I serve my customers who are doing business with me."

"Then you are able to go out for dinner every night leaving behind your wife and child?"

"I am doing business."

"There happens one week that all the 7 nights in that week you do not have dinner at home. All these nights you have dinners in restaurants."

"I have business customers."

"There is a rumour that you have a mistress who has a daughter with you. Is it correct?"

"Rubbish! Completely rubbish!"

"Why do you marry Terri?"

"We are introduced by Relau."

"Then you marry?"

"Of course."

"How long do you know Terri?"

"We go out together for a few months."

"Then get married?"

"Yes!"

"Do you love Terri?"

"Of course!"

"You love Terri then why you let her does housework not give her some help and even sit on sofa reading newspaper by yourself seems nothing has happened?"

"It is her job."

"Your job is to read newspaper?"

"What's the problem?"

"Do you actually know Terri?"

"Yes. Why?"

"You know she is submissive then you cheat her. Why you marry Terri is all because Relau is a wealthy man. You wish to give Relau a good impression together to show to your father you listen to elders not only lusts your father's money that you obey his words. Is it correct?"

"No, nonsense."

"A word to jury. I want to ask jury can we trust what Leather just said? Are these worth to give him a record of 'Good Man' or we tell him he is a 'Hypocrite'?"

"Why don't you move out?"

"I cannot support my own family."

"You do not go to work outside in other offices starting from an office boy waiting a chance to be promoted and in the meantime go to learn skills to develop your career. This is all because you listen to your father and you show your father you are a good son."

"……………"

"Before your marriage you let some people leaked an information to Terri that you are frightened of your father. This is to imply you always listen to your father. This is the only reason why."

"……………"

"You show to your father you obey him and never ever to put your wife as first priority. Is it correct?"

"Yes, absolutely."

"Then why your mistress's affidavit tells the court when you were chasing her you told her you would listen to her on any matter and you were prepared to be her slave?"

"No such thing."

"No such thing. Really?"

"Of course."

"How did you chase your mistress, then?"

"I offered her a house."

"Only this?"

"Yes."

"There is an incident that on that half a year you went to Planet #404 frequently on every 6 or 7 weeks at that period of time. You told your family it was all because of business. Is that correct?"

"Yes, absolutely."

"When I go to Planet #404 I find out at that time your mistress was having a baby girl and you are her biological father. Is that correct?"

"No, nonsense."

"Nonsense. How did that girl come to this world then?"

"I don't know."

"You definitely know Mr. Leather but you pretend not knowing the truth."

"I don't know."

"You tell your wife you want a fostered girl and that baby girl is your target when you migrated overseas right over here to reside. Unfortunately, that girl did not turn up and the idea is called off. Do you agree?"

"No, completely rubbish."

"May be that girl is another man's biological daughter, Mr Leather! But you are still in the cross-road!"

"I want to ask the Jury. Regarding to what Mr. Leather has said so far does the jury believe in his words or still puzzling? Or still in cross puzzle? Can we trust what he has said? The question is his art of telling lies and pretend to be a good man is so good that he is able to become the 'best shooting star' on these subjects. Or he is the best champion of the champions. Please give a verdict to this Hypocrite, Jury."

Later again in the court room,

"Mr Leather do you always go to your mother-in-law's retail shop to pick up, not to buy but pick up fruits for your own family celebration?"

"Yes, I do."

"Why don't you pay?"

"We are relatives. Why should I pay?"

"Is it correct that you need not pay?"

"Of course!"

"Why then when you borrowed money from your brothers-in-law. They told you to pay interest on top of the principle?"

"They are businessmen."

"Your mother-in-law is not a business woman?"

"She does not know what to do business."

"Then you are very good at doing business?"

"Of course."

"Why do you have not sufficient money to spend?"

"I need to go out with friends to dinner."

"This is business?"

"Yes it is."

"What business is this?"

"To say hello!"

"To say hello and you used up all your salary?"

"This is social gathering."

"You go to your mother-in-law's house to have dinner. Is it social gathering?"

"Of course."

"Why do you always curse her sons?"

"They are naughty."

"You expend vigorously to leave not a penny in the pocket. Then you borrow money. Is it mean that you are a good son?"

"……………….. To do business will have profit and loss."

"Not enough money is a loss in business?"

"Yes."

"Your idea is really innovative!"

At later life why Leather hates Tense so much? When Tense had an affair with Ellen. Tense on one night quarrelled with Leather and said something to insult Leather. Leather is a mean person. Even his blooded brothers to assault Leather, Leather is going to insult and humiliate whenever Leather has got a chance. As stated Leather and Little have a power struggle. Later on when another brother Letton refuses to listen to Leather and not helping Leather. Leather curse the brother every time Tense refuses to help Leather to let them as a scape-goat. These are good blooded brothers and sisters! God!

Lance also insulted Leather before but Leather still likes this son. Why? Simply Lance is able to help Leather to do business. How about Tense? Tense is only to answer phone calls or goes to a bank to deposit money or collect a cheque book. That's it! Not to let Tense to go to study nor go out to work will let Tense has no friends to give aids to Tense whenever Tense is in real trouble! The only option is turn to Leather for help! That means to beg Leather and his siblings. Never ever able to stand up as a man anymore!

Secondly, when Tense has got a little bit of super-natural feeling. Leather is very happy and tells everyone he meets. Simply Leather has face and tries to create chaos by letting other people jealous at Tense and harm Tense. Leather is able to come to help as a good father. Once a person asks Leather to help. Leather says 'Yes'. Before this happens Tense has already got a message that it is a crime if help is given. Tense is very annoyed after Leather mentions this aid meanwhile Leather shows an arrogant attitude that is to show Tense that Leather is not begging Tense but Tense still has to help.

Later on when Tense returns to good mood. Leather tries to find a chance to let Tense say something. Hoping a good news! Tense has got a feeling of what to answer or say before Tense sees Leather in the bedroom or toilet. While Tense is talking and then comes to this issue. Tense says, "It is you promise the person. It is then your job to do it yourself for him!" After hearing this Leather is very angry because Leather is not able to do it. Besides this Leather has no face as he promised and now cannot go on. Thus, Leather is very annoyed but says nothing. Meanwhile Leather is conspiring a retaliation. Again Leather needs Tense's help to accomplish Leather's gain of more power and reputation.

Another reason why Leather seduces Tense to work in LL. It is to control his uncle Less. After Laws's death Less did not expel Leather out of the family business. Leather does not know why at first! Later Leather finds out that it is because of Tense. It is Tense's future that Less is scared and obliged to let Leather stayed in another family business to work not manager any more.

After Laws's death there is a man arguing with Less. The man says, "Less, I need to remind you. You do not put the corpse of Laws in a coffin after his death for so many days. It will give an excuse in the future that Laws's decedents (implies Tense) come back to take on a revenge!" This man has said this. Is he on Leather's side? God knows! On Laws's side? God knows!

This is the reason why Leather tries every method to let Tense goes into LL to work as a clerk not manager. After Tense has worked for a few months. Leather curses Less every single matter Less did in front of Tense. Meanwhile there is a man who sits in the family office as visitor for many months. Whenever there is work or carpentry work needed to be done by the employees. This man, Ha, urgently helps to fulfil the jobs. This man wants to find a job in the Lung family business. Leather finds out this then immediately to upgrade the matter. Always yelling that Ha wants to work in the family company. Later Ha is working there.

Leather is already having left the family company. No matter what this man is doing. To find a job or to sit and talk. It is none of your business. What and where is your business? You are already thrown out of the family business. By now you still shout aloud saying this and that?

Hey, are you in charge of the business, man? If not, why do you always troubling the running of the business? You are not the boss nor even an employee in the business. But you shout and yell. Hey man, mind your own business!

Regarding this incident Leather has one more excuse to defame Less. It is very sure that Less will show his face to Ha. Simply Ha is begging Less for a job. Leather uses this chance, a real evidence, to defame Less whenever Leather has got his chance.

Why Laws hates Leather so much? Besides Leather is a playboy. Leather is not willing to go out to work to establish his business empire. Instead Leather stays in the family business as a boss to shout at employees and show off as a boss in front of other people especially his enemies and the people he hates.

Laws was an office boy as stated. Laws worked in an ancient style business bank for may be 10 years or so. In this working period Laws saw many types of people. The bad boys who played ladies and expended all his father's fortune. The women who gambled and lost all saving money and has not enough money to support the family as her husband went to sea as a sailor. These women came to the bank to borrow money. Also those people who cheated other people's money where they had some savings in the bank and those really worked hard to come to the bank to ask for a loan to do business. These bad people never ever paid back their loan but the good ones. All these types of people Laws saw a lot during his working period.

Again there were a few years Laws went on business with his wife's brother Mr Ting. As Tense understands

Laws is not educated. On their business transaction period there might be not sometimes but all the times Laws asked Ting what was the meaning of the word written on a billboard, on a poster or on the business contract. By this Laws gradually built up his knowledge. This is the reason why Tense sees there are newspaper in Laws's drawers inside his bedroom.

Laws's childhood might be not so good. His mother liked the younger son and let him to go to school. Not Laws. His father, as Tense understands, is a secret supplier to militia to resist the invasion of his home country. He died 3 months before the end of the war. Later on Laws's wife died. His wife liked Leather. It is why Leather was so cruel to his siblings at infancy which created so many turmoils and disputes and chaos in the family besides Leather and his mother's nasty personal characters.

At later life staying as a single parent with these money lusts children. Together with their waste spending of money and no one works in other business but only aim at the family business hoping to get some advantages. Hypocrisy among siblings. And always lied to Laws to exchange for his love to grab more money after his death. What can Laws say? What can he do? How can he solve these problems? Give them money no matter how much they want? Laws is not the government office where the paper money is printed. Nor he is the person who can do anything as he likes. Poor Laws!

But Laws, may be, inherited from his father. Laws usually donates money to charity. He also cooks some edible food to those refugees every morning at his home town. But Laws you have no luck! Your luck will come at your second life, Laws! Take care!

Among all these misfortunes Laws's only hope, may be, may be only on Tense. But Tense is not happy with the family. Also the family members always cheat Tense. May be Fairy's idea that Laws has another grandson who was born after Laws's death. This grandson wants to set up a business empire. Can he do it? It all depends on Laws's kind generosity to people and charity. May be 'Yes' or may be 'No'? Who knows?

One morning Leather is bringing Tense and Lance to the office. When they are crossing the road Leather says quietly, "Uncle Letton cannot complete his study on Planet #61. At that time the Lung family is still on Planet #77. Leather is happy that Letton cannot finish high school on Planet #61. Simply it is not Leather being sent by Laws to study on Planet #61. Leather jealous at Letton and Leather is also narrow-minded. Leather always says his siblings are good people because Leather watches them from childhood and Leather looks after them on the period they grow up. Oh, God! Why don't you say something? Our Almighty God!

Once Terri is having conversation and talking to Tense. Terri says Leather told Terri at that incident while Laws was walking very fast along the road. Laws told Leather to carry a large box of plates and cups followed behind Laws. Leather was chasing behind with a heavy box but Laws did not look at him but walked very fast. Leather used to tell people his father Laws is not good at him. Why Leather still obeys Laws? It is all because of Laws's money. Leather even blamed and lied to Terri that before Terri's marriage with Leather. Leather was the beloved son of Laws. God!

In the final 10 years of Laws's life it is all misfortunes coming and coming. These omens are mainly from inside the family.

First Laws has a disease of brain cancer. Laws is very scary and does not know what to do. Leather brings Laws to consult many doctors. One of the Medical Doctors tells them. Not to be frightened. It does not matter. Stay as you are until the moment you die. Not operated a surgery is better than one has done. This theory takes Laws's life. Around 10 years later Laws really dies.

After the discovery of cancer there is the new born baby grandson Lance. Lance is a naughty boy and getting worse and worse. Laws has no options but to bring Lance to go out to buy sweets to Lance and together visiting Laws's friends. These may be not really friends. In conversations with his friends Laws tries to speak in a manner to let Lance to go to the right path. This is Laws's only trick. At this time of the year Lance indeed thinks in the way of righteousness. In later life Lance is influenced by Leather and uncles and aunts to go the wrong way. Leather knows Lance loves money. It is the trick Leather uses to put Lance in high reputation and wealthy. Not a single cent to Tense. They fail. All good members of the family turn to Tense before they die. Tense has some supporters in the family. Later it is because Leather is losing power and influence and target is to destroy Tense. Hence, Leather tells these supporters that Tense is mad and not to trust Tense. This is the last resort that Leather has in order to re-gain power and influences. Finally, the supporters all die in an incredible accidental scene. Leather immediately blames Tense that it is done by Tense. A father. A son! Stupid son!

Another problem comes from the family business. The other 2 brother partners join together to quarrel with Laws and provide false evidence that Laws has spent too much. Then Laws has only got a fixed amount of money every month to expend. This is financial restriction to control Laws. His brothers use this trick all the time. One more nasty joke is the brother always needs his supporters to betray their own biological parents and blooded brothers and sisters. Then at this moment he believes the person is loyal to him.

These 2 brothers quarrel with Laws and at that time Laws may have regrets that why at the first stage Laws allowed his brothers to be partners in his company where this company is established by Laws himself with many hardships and setbacks at onset. At that time might be because they are brothers. To show to mother we are really good brothers and sons. Then they are partners in the company. God! Why it happened? See? Now? What is happening?

After the death of Laws these 2 brothers and their families went broke and remained poor until all decedents died. Is this Fairy's verdict? God's will? From drama movies there is always a dialogue saying, "If you do so many evil things in your life. You are certain to get penalty from Heaven on yourself. If not, the penalty will be placed on your offspring.". Do you believe in it? Is it trustworthy? Who knows? God!

The last time Laws is in hospital the doctor in charge is a nonsense. Laws dies finally. Afterwards Leather used to say this Dr Good has good reputations but his patients all say he is no use. Leather stays in the family office for 20 or 30 years. He always tells people especially Terri that after the first conversation with anybody. Leather is able to identify the person is good or bad. But now Leather does not know the Dr Good is bad. Why? Ask him yourself! No jokes!

Later on, Lance turns out to be an omen and goes to the wrong path. This is not what Laws wants to see! But what? If Laws is still alive. What will he say? Or what can he say? What can he do? After the deaths of all these nasty people. What can they say to their father when they are all in Hell? They must have a long meeting or long argument. Are they able to argue over Almighty God? Tell me, please! Don't forget there is a Last Judgement Day!

At the time Leather was a wealthy son and Leather always said this person is no good and the doctor who was introduced by Leather's friend Mr. Bead made a mistake that Leather had to have a needle every day in the doctor's clinic. But no one argues with Leather. After Laws was dead Leather has no money and no influence in family and family business. From then on all Leather's friends curse Leather. Leather at this moment is like a dog. It is why Leather hates his uncle or Laws's brother Lave so much. At the later life Leather uses all possible tricks to push down Lave as revenge.

Look at Leather's brothers and sisters. Just from above his brother Letton and another sister Lie. As stated she loves power and money. While Tense is young and a favourite grandson and a favourite son to be loved by anybody. Lie uses all opportunities and methods to have Tense's favour towards Lie. Every time Leather buys a for example, a new watch or necklace to Tense. Lie used to scream loud, "Tense you have a gold watch and a new gold necklace. Lance you have got nothing!".

These expressions are always to stir up hatred between Tense and Lance. To create disputes and turmoils. At later time, or Leather is always, as stated above Leather tells Tense that, "These brothers and sisters are brought up partly by myself. I watch them to grow up from infancy to adulthood. They are good brothers and sisters!"

Oh! My God! Leather's brothers and sisters are good people. While Terri's brothers and sisters are bad sons and bad daughters. How do you deduce this reasoning, man? All your deductions are correct which are as accurate as to the political leaders' decisions, right? If you are correct why your brothers and sisters not listen to you and even create a power struggle with you? Are you always right, man? Of course you are not, man! You are a hypocrite! You manage affairs only to your own benefits! You even say or curse your brother who once told you, "I will stand by the side that benefits me!" or your uncle Less's responses to those not listen to Less by the method of economic sanctions simply not distribute the dividends to family members in order to control the family members all to listen to Less! Are you doing the same now? What do you do to Tense? You do not give him money (while Tense is happy with this) and control him not to work in offices and not to study in colleges that is certain to have Tense's own friends. Whenever Tense has problems Tense has to turn to you for aids! What cunny it is, man? You are the same product of your brothers and uncles, man! Are you not? If you are not, prove it! Alternatively, you are a Buddha follower. Swear to Buddha, man! Are you able to do this, man?

Lie creates all these disputes between Tense and Lance. At later life Lie does not do this to her own son, Loft. Instead Lie treats Loft as best as she can. Buy any new things to Loft such as a new piano, new clothes and everything is new. Besides these once when Tense is asking to buy a new violin for musical lessons. It is told by the coach to buy a new violin. But Leather pretends not to trust Tense and calls to Lie. Lie screams over the phone, "It is definitely not necessary!" What are you doing now?

Tense once tells Leather in a letter saying, "Everything I did, do and will do are all according to my conscience. Not a single tiny matter is against my conscience." As Tense watches movies once said in the dialogue, "If I do not commit crime. I am able to talk to the judges. I am not scary to talk and I have courage to confess I have done nothing wrong. I do not need to hide or conceal what I have done. Simply I commit no crimes!"

At later life Lance still assumes Lie is good to him. Lance always does anything to help Lie. Lie even gives the baby bed to Lance's new born baby to simply say she is good to Lance. Stupid boy! Lance even does all his best to against Terri to stand by the side of Lie. Bad son and inhuman! Remember what they did when Terri was young, man? What you are doing now is to give Fairy an excuse or pretext to punish you! It's up to you. You did it and you deserved it!

CHAPTER 3

When Tense is in another new elementary school once he suddenly has an idea. It is to learn martial arts. Tense tells this secret to his best friend Gogo. A few days later Gogo asks there is any new news or not. Tense says there is no martial arts master. On the same night while both of them are travelling back home from school. Gogo points to a martial arts school to Tense. The following day Gogo asks for good news. Tense replies that his father disagrees. Leather wants Tense to study hard to achieve good academic results such that Leather can show off. This makes Tense being diagnosed a fatal illness some time later in his life. But Leather finds an excuse that Leather wants Tense becomes a skilled professional. In such case there is no need to study in a famous school as in the meantime Leather is trying to send Tense to famous university on a planet somewhere over there in the Galaxy. This idea is dropped after Tense diagnosed as neurological patient because of tense academic assignments.

In this new college it is the onset of Tense's real life experience to see the ugliness of mankind and dirty sides of this society. As in later life Leather isolates Terri and Tense not to let them go out nor study nor even to work on a job. Also in this college Tense meets his good friend who always helps Tense that Tense owes him a debt in later life. This boy Gogo always advises Tense on any difficult issue Tense is facing and always initiate to help Tense. Even Gogo's mother has a very good impression on Tense and always welcomes Tense to go out with Gogo whenever Gogo tells her.

In the first year of this college there is already problems. First one afternoon during arithmetic class Tense needs to go to bathroom. He tells the class-mistress and stays on toilet for 10 or 20 minutes. It is the time the class-mistress sends the boy sitting next to Tense to call him back. But Tense is in trouble because there is no toilet paper. When Tense returns to classroom every class-mate laughs at him. God!

Events on later years of this elementary school will be discussed later. It is from this college St Joseph College that begins the troubled life of Tense for more than 40 years. The principle Kwok only lusts for power, influence and reputation. He forces every student to study hard to achieve his aim to let the College becomes famous and also himself.

It is on the second last year that Tense stays is the onset of the struggle. In this year Tense wants to chase a girl Ellen. This Ellen is a snake. She also lusts for power and reputation. Same character as Kwok. When Tense first know her. She is applying for university study. It is because of her examination results are bad but she insists to go into university. Ellen discusses with her father who is a working staff in university. Ellen uses the pretext that Tense chases her. She tells everyone that she is able to tell. This is to tell or show her ability to become Tense's girlfriend. (At that time Tense does not realise his affair is gossiped by everyone who knows it). By this Ellen is admitted to university as stated somewhere in this story.

In the long struggle with Kwok Tense realises Kwok's cruel managements towards students which Tense heard from other school-mates some time at earlier grades. Kwok first keeps Tense stays in College to let Tense to repeat. This is the third time in grade 9 plus one year in hospital. This means it is totally four years on this grade already. Then the College changes its policy. The class timetable is changed to 10 lessons each day for 5 days. Saturdays are now school holidays. In the past students attended class for 9 lessons every day and half a day every Wednesday and Saturday.

What is the purpose to change? It is to damage Tense neurological ability to let Tense goes back to hospital. But why? The day when Tense was previously discharged from hospital. Tense forgot some of the past events. Kwok wants Tense to be re-admitted to hospital and forgot his quarrel with Kwok. Or it is saying that may be Tense pretends to forget in order to receive once again his power Kwok has given him before.

Tense understands this and tells himself to get over it in order to win. In the second half of this grade Tense has a schedule as to work hard in summer holidays then promoted to grade 10 and passes the final examination and be admitted to another elementary school instead of Kwok's. Tense has already borrowed note-books from other class-mates ready for the holiday. Finally, Tense is expelled from College. Why Kwok suddenly does it?

Before Tense's expulsion Kwok as mentioned in the story tries 3 times to show his concerns in Tense. He walks out of his office to look down to play grounds to see students playing. This is always done by Tense and this event happens two times. But Tense does not know this. Only after Kwok goes back to his office that other students tell Tense. The third or final time is Kwok stands at the class room entrance to watch Tense writing notes dictated from the Biology teacher.

This time Tense has some feelings that something is happening and decides to look up but he does not even the teacher comes close to his desk and says 'good'. This is told by Kwok actually. Is it not? It is also that Tense found out what is going on by his class-mate sitting next to him after Kwok's departure.

It is because of these 3 incidents that Kwok could not contact Tense. Kwok decides to ask Leather to his office to pick up Tense's academic results. Also Kwok advises Leather if Tense has got good results in other elementary school outside. Kwok is always welcome his return. But one thing Kwok does not know. It is in Leather's mind he is figuring his plan to gain power, influences and reputations by using Tense to stay under Leather's control not Kwok's.

At last Tense goes to another elementary school to study. In this year it is a good year. Ellen's men cannot join the school as students such as to disturb Tense to study and force Tense to return to St Joseph. Also in this year Tense has a year of peace to recover from his illness and get ready for further education.

It is after Tense leaves this school that begins Tense's difficult life journey that sometimes discourages Tense.

Before going to another secondary school. On this summer vacation Tense goes to biology class on university campus. Sometimes go to picnic with the student teachers and 1 or 2 classmates. In this holiday Tense does anything is abnormal. First he always goes out to lunch or dinner. He goes out every day sometimes till to 10pm to arrive back home. On Tense behalf he really wants to revise all lessons before going back to St Joseph where Kwok is school principal. Why?

After discharged from hospital Tense was told by Leather to consult an acupuncture practitioner. This happens before the struggle with Kwok. At first stage it seemed quite alright. After 6 months it was going wrong. Tense's responses to outside stimuli was from bad to worse. At that time Tense used to feel sleepy after dinner. At this time Tense is going to revise but fell asleep up to 10 or 11pm and then went to bed to sleep. This happens at the time when Tense returns to St Joseph after the summer vacation.

In the holiday Tense is worse than before. At this time Tense had the affair with Ellen that caused Tense had no time to rest and to think about what he was going to do.

When school year re-starts Tense goes back to St Joseph and 2 months later returns to medical tablets instead. But Tense really has to thank the acupuncture practitioner of his help and his wife's aids during the summer vacation to stand behind Tense to fight against Kwok. After returning to medical tablets Tense becomes inert and every night stays before TV set to watch television without saying a word nor even go to bathroom but stays on sofa up to 10 or 11 pm then goes to sleep. It lasts until the end of school year that Tense is transferred to St Antony.

In this year Ellen has already contacted the teachers in St Joseph to keep an eye on Tense as Kwok is cruel to the teachers thus, they turn back at Kwok. On the whole year Tense is inert and without any active behaviours nor even not takes part in physical education lessons as much as possible. Then one school year has elapsed and Tense becomes a little bit active. He even tries to walk to St Antony from his home to see how far it is in order to prepare to walk to school and walk back home in the new school year.

As Tense recalls this last year in St Joseph is a year of nonsense. Tense did not know what was going on instead just went to school and returned home to watch television. Also in this year two female teachers competing to give a good impression to Tense. Lazy is a bit better and shows some concerns on Tense. The other one Assay is a snake. Assay used to say something that will stir up a quarrel between Tense and Leather. To conclude to study in this school is similar to take part in a society earning your livelihood. There are turmoils, chaos and disturbances happened whenever and wherever you are in. No difference!

After Tense's departure from St Joseph and studying in St Antony. Leather has a plan to chase for more reputations and influences. First Leather hinders Tense's desire to return to St Joseph. Then Leather is waiting for any opportunity to transfer Tense to another school where Leather is able to put his conspiracy into action.

Fortunately, Leather has got a chance. It is because the teachers in St Antony are in chaos. The teachers there all only work for 1 or 2 years then resign to other profession. The school principal wants to invite the teachers to stay in his school for a longer time. The principal Woo realises Tense is a great man, if he is, in future. He finds out at the stadium where they are having sports day. Then Woo tells all staffs while these employees split into 2 groups. One opposes the other. One group is controlled by the 3 influential teachers. The other group members are new teachers just begin teaching in that year or the year before.

At the end of the school year the influential group decides to oblige Tense to repeat. Tense refuses and moves to Lees College arranged by Leather. Later on Tense finds out principal Woo moves to live in another country while the influential teachers either leave the school or stay there without any power.

From this time onwards Leather pretends to be a good man and a good father in front of all people. Actually some of these intellectual teachers realise Leather's tricks but not say a word and resign at the end of the school year.

Leather pretends not knowing Tense's matters outside home. That means he does not know the case of Ellen. Then from the teachers in Lees he finds out the girl Ellen is disturbing Tense from that time. Tense stays in this College for 4 or 5 years but still does not know this Leather's dirty trick. Ellen has been disturbing Tense 3 or 4 years before Tense attends Lees. Leather pretends not know anything about it. In fact, Leather knew this girl Ellen well before. In that summer holiday Leather discussed with Kwok on how to call Tense back to St Joseph and how to split Tense and Ellen.

The principal Kwok always shows his keen concerns on Tense. Also worry about Tense's future and wants Tense to become a leader sometime later in his life as expected by Kwok. Will Tense become a great man for all times? All these are real or invalid seems watching an actor performing his/her show in an opera on stage? Look at this!

When Tense is in dispute with Kwok regarding the chasing of Ellen. Kwok tries every single chance to destroy this affair and still wants Tense to stay in St Joseph. Fortunately, Tense returns. It is a different story! In this year Kwok tries many methods to make Tense returns to hospital as stated. Another issue is there is a boy in Tense's class named Banman. It is a rumour that his father betrayed his home country while the country was under invasion. True or not find it out yourself, man!

Tense never ever talks to Banman and Banman is now class 11. Two classes higher than Tense at the time. If Kwok is good to Tense why Kwok allows Banman to be a prefect in charge of the other students whenever these students break school rules? Also to let Banman to be a prefect means other students cannot quarrel or curse Banman as the son of a betrayer. Of course, Kwok first told Banman not to disturb Tense. But what is the point to put Banman on top of Tense on the first place? It also makes Banman stays above other students and control other students. Again Banman's father is a man of ill-reputation at that time around the college. Kwok still promote Banman to be a prefect. What is going on there? Is this a good sign Kwok wants to show Tense? Tell me, man!

When Leather goes to Lees to register for Tense to go into the College. Leather is able to catch a cab but instead Leather catches a mini-bus. Why? Leather wants the Ellen followers to dog where Leather is going. When they find out. Ellen can send the boys to Lees to disturb Tense. At that time Leather is able to become a good father and a good man in front of many teachers and the Directors of Lees College who comes from a wealthy family. Again these Directors are friends of Leather at that time interval! Simple!

These 5 years in Lees Tense meets different boys sent by Ellen to study in Lees every year. These boys disturb the College functioning and disturb Tense's academic results in order to let Tense returns to St Joseph where Ellen has influences. They do not give the examination timetable to Tense as to let Tense fails in all the subjects. Unfortunately, Tense is admitted into a private university to study economics. But Ellen still keep doing on her ugly cunny tricks to disturb Tense's attendance and let Tense returns to St Joseph.

It is because this first year in this university Louise which Tense's application is a sudden move without early indications. Tense suddenly finds out that Louise is recruiting new students on a Saturday morning. Then goes to apply and is accepted as student. In the entrance examination Tense cannot write down more than one sentence on the answer sheet of a composition as required but passes. First, it is Ellen has bad university results and her admission to university is introduced by her father such that Ellen does not want other people to tease her. Then she persuades Louise to accept Tense even without writing anything on answer sheet. Secondly, Louise wants to teach Tense not lazy but work hard. Hence, in the interview the principal asks Tense. Tense replies he wants to focus on economics study.

In this year Tense works very hard and answer all questions in examinations correctly but got a low pass mark. Later Tense migrates overseas but does not ask for academic reports. As Tense thinks they won't give Tense a good result. Also Tense is not planning to study after migration but to work from low position. Indeed, if Tense actually asks for the results from Louise. Tense may get a very good mark instead. Who knows? We now stop right here and continue later!

It happens all the time. Whenever Leather and Terri go out to dinner at night Tense is very worry. At that time Tense is only 6 or 7 years old. At one night before going out Leather asks Tense for the reason. Tense says he is afraid of Galaxy War. Leather calms Tense down by saying if there is Galaxy War Leather will not go out but stay home. From then on Tense plays happily with the younger brother every time his parents go out.

One night when Tense and Lance are home while their parents are out for dinner. Tense remembers he is not allowed to learn martial arts. Tense got an idea that he himself can create his own style of martial arts. Immediately Tense sits down on a sofa to figure a series of martial arts movements. Only seconds later Tense tells himself he is not a master then he cannot create his own style and he is not able to fight others or his enemies with his stupid martial arts fighting styles. Then Tense puts down his pen and watches television.

One day it is Sunday when Tense plays with Lance while Leather and Terri are out. They learn from television series to fight each other. Meanwhile Tense tells Lance to hit his face same as in the series. Lance hits Tense's stomach which makes him very painful. After this incident for a few months Tense used to have stomach ache. Leather always says as excuse it is Tense that eats too much or too quick. Always finds excuses not to pay doctor's fee in order to save money. This is the character of Leather's family. From then on Tense is troubled with his stomach ache for another 5 years or so only later to find out it is because of the impairment under neurological deficiency. The disease is all because of too much pressure on academic assessments and the elementary school teachers to give home works and tests every day.

Why does it happen? The principal uses the pretext that it is government's policy to urge school children to achieve high examination results in order to go to secondary schools. The real reason is the principal wishes his/her students to obtain good marks in such a case the principal is famous and many children go to apply in that elementary school. It is all for the good advantages of the principal. Nothing else.

This principal always argue it is government's policy. In those other not famous schools the school principal and teachers give students home works only urge students to work hard but few tests. Some students tell themselves to obtain a good mark and they succeed. No need to put pressure on them. A great idea!

After a few years when Tense grows older while he is sleeping on his bed. Tense thinks of grandfather Laws. Tense thinks if Laws dies what happens to Tense then? At that time Tense has tears down from his eyes. After that night Tense forgets everything. Two years later Laws dies and Tense is in a difficult and series condition.

At a later time in a law firm a barrister comments,

Under these circumstances Tense's General Practitioner makes the conclusion about Tense's characters is quite alright. The doctor deduces that Tense is very pure and that's why the doctor wants to teach him hatred. By doing this Tense has to remind himself all the time that not every person is a good person. Again not every person does a wrong thing afterwards they will genuinely repent.

But on second thought is Tense actually of purity. No one knows. It is only the doctor's deduction. Who knows? It all needs Tense's friends in his later life to put a conscience comment. Alternatively, no one agrees. Who knows?

Before these happen Terri is in hospital. At that time Leather pretended to visit Terri on Saturdays and Sundays. Pretended to be a good husband. During weekdays Leather brings Tense and Lance to office room. Leather works and both children play especially Lance.

After lunch Tense goes to school while Lance stays behind. It is later Tense deduces that many afternoons

Laws brings Lance to go out most of the times. To buy sweets or other chocolates to Lance. Lance is very happy.

At this time Tense suddenly figures out his mother is in hospital. Tense decides to write letters to Terri. Meanwhile Lance asks Terri to write down both names. Once or twice Lance wants his name to be written first. Tense is happy to do that. But when all are written down properly. A man tells Tense that he is elder than Lance that's why his name should be written first. Tense then writes a new copy but does not observe Lance's response. Maybe Lance is not happy or maybe. Who knows?

In later years when Terri is talking to Tense. Terri tells Tense when she was in hospital Leather threatened to divorce her but later called off this idea. Why Leather called off? No one knows! Maybe threatened Terri not to blame Leather's brothers and sisters. Maybe to control Terri after discharged from hospital that she has still to do house work. Maybe fear Laws is not happy then Leather calls off this threat. At later time during conversation Tense tells Terri that Leather is playing Terri from the very beginning. Leather actually does not love Terri at all. These can be proved by Leather's later attitudes and conducts towards Terri after marriage.

Terri says to Tense once when Terri is very annoyed and Terri goes back to her parents' premises. After 1 or 2 months when Terri is calmed down. Leather rings to Terri to say nothing not even an apology but to tell Terri to return his home and do all house work as usual.

Leather is no regret and is of no conscience. Does Leather love Terri? Who knows? Tense's viewpoint is

Leather does not love Terri up to the time of Leather's death. Hypocrite only plays ladies.

Leather tells and shows other people he is a faithful religious follower of B religion. But Leather never goes to worship monastery also never says any prayers. But only gives some money to the monks in the New Year. Leather gives $1,000 to the monks.

Later on Terri tells Tense that Leather only gives $10 to Leather's parents-in-law. Leather never ever calls nor greets his parents-in-law. Leather goes to his parents-in-law's home only to eat those most expensive food which requires heavy preparations. Terri's mother cooks the food and washes them in cold water in winter. Leather only eats and goes there to curse the brothers-in-law to express Leather's anger after his work in the family office.

After Tense was born up to Tense's age of 12 it is Tense's climax of his life. On academic life and one private life. Tense is rewarded with second in arithmetic's in class 4. Also second in language in class 5. Becomes 5th of the whole class in class 6. Finally, becomes 4th in the class in class 7. But after these glorious days Tense's fortune is going downslope started from the death of Laws. Laws's death is a suddenly appears to happen that Tense never expects this. It is the bad news suddenly comes forwards without any warning.

After becomes the 4th in class many girls play and talk to Tense. Tense is very happy because there is fun. What Tense knows is they are all playing and having fun with Tense and does not realise any secrets of the girls. A teacher an old woman sees this and she tells herself quietly

Tense is foolish but not in his study. Tense does not know any secrets from the start to the end.

Also because of this happening a classmate is jealous and hates Tense. Kee starts to defame Tense in front of other students. This is the reason why no one talks or plays with Tense. From then on Tense begins his lonely life. A lonely boy! It is said to be fortunate or unfortunate that Tense can lead a lonely life to solve problems and burdens from then on by himself without outside aids. Lucky for him it is done in himself only! And only Tense can do anything by himself alone which other people cannot!

As stated before,

In the court room,

"Mr. Leather do you recall that every time you go to your mother-in-law's house you have quarrels with your brothers-in-law and sisters-in-law?"

"Yes, I remember these clearly."

"Why do you argue with them?"

"They are naughty boys. They oppose their mother, not listen to her."

"Then you curse them?"

"Of course."

"Why do you do these?"

"They are bad sons and bad daughters."

"You are a good son, aren't you?"

"Of course I am."

"You do not move out from family house in order to work in your father's office. Your father and uncle tell you to arrive office room before 9:00am and also stay in office on Sundays. It means you cannot return home to see your wife and children. This is a good son's behaviour?"

"I must obey my father."

"You curse your brothers-in-law. How about their mother Tane? Does she say anything?"

"No, she doesn't."

"But you always curse them?"

"Yes, of course."

"What is your position in the family?"

"I am their brother-in-law."

"You curse them meanwhile their mother says nothing?"

"Yes."

"Do they have other brother-in-law?"

"Yes, there is."

"What does he do? Does he curse them?"

"No, he doesn't."

"But you curse your brothers-in-law?"

"........................"

"Do they fight back?"

"No."

"It is because you are a wealthy son. They need to listen to you?"

"..............................."

"After your father's death you lose everything. What do they do?"

"They trap me nearly to be a gaol."

"Why do they do these?"

"..............."

"Jury, I need to convince the jury. When Mr. Leather is a wealthy son having all the things he wants. At that time period he stays in materialism. Mr. Leather curses his friends and curses those brothers-in-law. Meanwhile when he loses power and has no money. He always quarrels with his uncle showing he is the deputy manager to recover his power. His uncle harms him not giving him much family fortunes. He is a slave at that time.

"I want to ask Jury. What can we say or comment on his behaviours and manners towards other people especially those from poverty? Mr. Leather even he himself does not give money to beggars on New Year day. Not a single cent to be honest! Is this generosity or dictatorship? Is he kind hearted or a mean person?"

Leather even tells his siblings where Tense is also there, to say a good friend of Laws once praised Leather that he is a good husband caring for his wife Terri. Jesus Christ! In Leather's later life he is very sick and Terri and Tense both care for Leather. But Leather never ever says 'thank you' nor shows any happy face to both of them. Leather as usual eats and drinks when he is sick. While Tense is caring for him in Leather's later life when Leather is sick to serve him to bed. Leather asks Tense why the medication does not work? It's to let Tense to try his super natural feelings to find out why. Jesus, how are you?

By not doing as instructed from specialists and specially to eat fatty foods to make the heart disease even worse. All these are to let Tense stay with Leather in case something happens. Tense is ready to help. Or frankly, to control Tense not go out to work nor study but stay home that whenever Tense is having problems. Leather and his siblings are, pretend, ready to help. Then they are always on the top of the world. Jesus, please come back quicker!

Before Tense turns 15 these are the golden days of Tense and Leather, at least possibly. Leather always goes out to gamble and then dines with friends. At first Terri is not allowed to go. Leather's friend Mr. Chung always saying in front of all people present at the dinner table that no one is doing the same as Leather. Leather always goes out on his own and never ever brings his wife with him. Leather sits there and listens without saying a word. Then does as he does. Never repent nor feels guilty. Does Leather love Terri?

It is after the death of Laws. Leather is thrown out of the family office by his uncle Less. From that time onwards Leather loses everything. Money and power. But Leather still takes on his power struggle. Leather quarrels with Less every day in the office claiming the family business is founded by Laws. It is Less who eats up their shares and occupies all the family businesses. Stupid man. Who is going to give you back the shares in the company? If you were I, were you going to return money to your enemy who will become a threat in your later life?

When Tense turns 15 he is admitted to neurological clinic for 4 months under radiology treatment. From this incident onwards Leather is very good to Lance. Buys good food back home for the family and brings Lance to dinner whenever someone invites Leather.

Lance at this stage also is good to Tense. Once Tense gives delicious food to Lance. Lance says he always has that and returns to Tense at one dinner time. But Lance changes his attitude in his later life towards Tense. Lance becomes an alien monster with only hatred inside his body and blood and mind in order to commit whatsoever crimes he is able to as he will hopefully evade to be prosecuted.

Why Lance becomes such an inhuman? His grandfather Laws predicts and deduces this happening long and very long time ago. When Terri is in hospital Tense and Lance go to family office every day until late at night. During the afternoons Tense goes to study while Lance stays behind. In this period Laws always brings Lance to go outside buying sweets and other beverages to Lance. Laws talks to Lance on everything. Laws teaches him to be good no evils. Why? Laws was an office boy in an old fashioned bank when Laws was young before he starts his business as said before. On Laws's work he sees many people. All types of bad people, bad sons, gambling people, playing ladies and those bad sons and daughters who steal parents' money and flee away. Laws has encountered every single type of people in this world.

Laws deduces Leather will become a man that is intolerable in the future maybe after Laws's death. Laws is very scare Lance will follow his father's way of doing things. It is maybe this reason Laws teaches Lance all types of good conducts. Why? Because Laws knows Lance's characters are on the borderline between good and bad. Lance is most probably influenced by bad people like Leather to do evil things. Laws has confidence on Tense but not Lance. Therefore, Laws does all he can do to help Lance. Fortunately, the weather forecast is accurate and Lance becomes an evil man offending anything he can in order to make himself good and have a better life with his own family. At later life he is also encouraged by his wife's ugly persuasion to commit omens.

From then on the two brothers never ever talk to each other anymore. Seems strangers not even let the other to go inside their home to sit down and talk or have a cup of tea.

Every night Laws goes back to family home to have a shower and his dinner. Laws watches his sons and daughters saying these saying those. His mother says who is good who is bad. Every single night Laws has the same experience. Laws knows his descendants are no good only lust his money. Perhaps because of this Laws intentionally not leaving his Last Will to let these people to fight for their lusts. Therefore, other people, relatives and their own friends will tease them. But no good, failed. They do as what they usually do!

CHAPTER 4

Looking back at Tense.

The first 12 months in Louise is not a good experience. Tense goes to lectures and back home. Tense has got the past 5 years-experiences in contact with Ellen's boys. Tense realises the classmates all know Tense's past experiences with Ellen but some are good students coming to learn and become good friends with Tense.

At the end of the academic year the classmates in History unit all agree to visit the Lecturer on a day but Tense does not attend to. On the Wednesday evening a student who wants to be friend with Tense. He intentionally waits at the College entrance to ask Tense the reason why as soon as Tense walks out of College to have dinner before lecture in the evening. This gentleman later, same as others, believes in Ellen's evil story and turns out to be alien with Tense.

What Ellen is talking about? The 5 years-study in Lees Tense only studies but repeat and repeat. Even Tense himself does not know why. It is later going to Louise. In this 5 years stay in Lees. Tense attends summer secretary class twice. The first time Tense secretly register without Ellen's notice.

Later on during the course Ellen got the message and sends her boys to study in the class but all are refused. Ellen has nothing to work on to harm Tense. Later on Ellen, Tense does not know how, contacts the teachers in the summer class by saying Tense is chasing her. Then she wants to keep an eye on Tense not to chase other girls. Ellen insists Tense is deeply in love with her. Then one afternoon after class Tense is trying to get a girl student's telephone number. In doing this what Tense thinks at the very starting point is not to let the teacher knows as students are asking questions at that time after class. But while Tense is talking to the girl. Another girl has finished her questions to the teacher and turns her body away after talking to the Indian teacher and the gap is big enough to let the teacher to see what Tense is doing. It is this incident that all people know Ellen is lying and refuse to trust her any more.

From then on what Ellen is talking will be she is deeply in love with Tense. On the contrary, Tense is a playboy always seduces other girls and deserts Ellen behind. The point is that Ellen is a good girl while Tense is a bad or very bad boy that no one likes Tense. The point is that Ellen loves Tense so much that Ellen will be upset once Tense leaves Ellen. Hence, Ellen will do her best to keep an eye on Tense and asks every person who is able to do something such that to help Ellen. In front of other people Ellen is a pure girl and also a revolutionist and is definitely going to help Tense in Tense's future life. All are absolutely nonsense! Completely rubbish! Better ask God that will God believe in what she says! Are they all lies? Ellen is a snake to lusts for power but a terribly stupid snake! Also ask Ellen does she believe herself in what she says?

At the end of school year there is an outing that many students join to participate. On the way returning home the travel coach stops for a while for some reasons. Then a girl walks from the back to where Tense is sitting to talk to Tense. She is holding a video game player. The next morning Tense wakes up and goes to purchase a video game player simply because Tense watches other people playing for a lot of times. Why Tense not purchase at that time is simply these only takes you to waste lots of your time and does you no good. You are wasting your time which is ready there to offer you sufficient time to study. But Tense buys it.

Then as usual Ellen spreads out the news in order to let Ellen on the commander position. Ellen says or lies that Tense loves the girl. It is only to buy a games machine. What's wrong with it? But Ellen creates this rumour and makes it a snow ball rowing bigger and bigger. This is to enhance her position as commander and to show people that Tense is a very bad boy while Ellen is a good and pure girl. Tense knows all these dirty tricks but doesn't utter a single word. Only after departure from Louise finally that Tense realises the Lecturers are good to Tense and they secretly destroy Ellen to push Tense back on track. It's too late, baby!

In these 5 or 6 years Ellen tries every single chance to humiliate Tense. Blames Tense as a lazy boy does not study hard, a playboy who plays girls, a boy who always does not non-conscience matters, a boy who deserts Ellen means Tense is not a real and good husband to rely on and everything Tense does is not to his conscience. By all these Ellen even tells a boy to humiliate Tense as a gay person by leaning to Tense's body on a seat on a bus. These are all lies and insults to Tense. Why Ellen has to do all these? It is because Ellen has to pretend as a good girl with purity in front of every other person all the time. Also to pretend to be a revolutionist to reform any government. Ellen hates Tense very much at that time period but she can say nothing simply Tense does not chase her and she has no good academic results in university. Indeed, she is stupid and narrow-minded that she even does not pass university examinations. Ellen needs to express her anger. The only option is Tense.

Whenever Tense has something done in gladness Ellen is sure to make it a tragedy by telephoning to Tense's home phone line to disturb Tense. No matter Tense has got some money or something like this. Ellen will send her man to curse Tense at his back while walking on the street. The men just say, "Likes money." While Tense has a chance that Tense might know another girl. These men say, "It is God's idea." Implying that Tense deserts Ellen but another boy falls in love with Ellen and they are good friends now.

These women and men who help Ellen is partly cheated by her family's wealth or simply her father is working in university and may have a high salary or have saved some money. Secondly it is Ellen's cheating skills is on top of the world. Ellen lies to anyone with a beautiful story. Later in life these followers turn to support Leather. It is all because that Ellen's family has no money any more. The saved money is all used by the son going overseas to study. The son may be having low assignments marks. Thus, he rings back home to his girlfriend frequently. Each time they talk on the phone for at least half an hour. Used up all the savings of the family. Simple as that!

The second reason is at that time Leather is a millionaire. It means he has money. Thus, the followers all turn to support Leather. Leather already knows this type of people but Leather has to use them as some hints in the future to fix into Leather's own conspiracy plan. Thus, Leather pretends not know what had happened or what was happening in Tense's study in Lees and Louise.

The point is while Tense is still staying in Lees. Leather acts like a good father always goes to the College to ask anything about Tense to know what is happening there. At this time Leather is already knowing there are followers. This can be proved by the partners in the company. At this time Leather's business is with partnership of Leather's paternal uncle Choy. Leather pretends to be a good man all the time. Simply to show to his uncle Choy and the Directors of Lees College as a good man deserved to be respected.

Meanwhile when Leather accepts these followers. At this time the company LL is dominated by Leather. His partner Lows knows nothing about business. It is Leather's conspiracy. That's why after 6 months Leather seduces Tense impliedly to work in LL. All people are saying the business will belong to Tense after Leather's death. Indeed, it is not. Leather already got a plan to do business to partner Lance. Thus, Tense does not hear any single word from Leather that he will give the business to Tense. Sometimes when Tense is speaking some other issues that might related to Leather's business or why Leather gives so much money to Lance to spend. Leather stays as usual very quiet and not utter a single word. It is because if Leather answers what Tense's questions are it will reveal Leather is a hypocrite and a big liar sometime in the future. This largely disturbs and destroys Leather's reputation and his long-time schedule as a gentleman in front of others.

Before the end of the first 2 months in second year study in Louise Tense is seduced by Leather to work in Leather's company LL where Leather is the big shareholder. Also from this time Tense loses his chance to study in university. Also from this time it is the onset of lots of sufferings to Tense that at the final series Tense is getting back his self-esteem and knows how stupid he was to trust Leather. Also from this period is the commencement of Tense's life journey especially later on after Leather's fatal death punished by Fairy! Also from this time onwards Tense realises the ugly faces of Leather's family where all members lust for money and power. Even sends their daughters to marry wealthy sons to push up their social status and gain more influences and power!

After the people follow Leather instead. Leather pretends not know anything happened before. Meanwhile these followers suggest to Leather that they detect Ellen's secret then to test Tense's response to see Tense is a good boy or not! Leather pretends very happy to have these people to help and support him. In the first 9 months in LL Leather always stirs up a quarrel with Tense while Tense is already in puzzle. Why Leather always curse me that I have always shown him I am good many times? Once at lunch on Sunday there is an interview with someone Tense does not know but he knows Tense's sad experiences in LL is being interviewed in a radio station. In the interview the man insists not to quarrel. After this lunch Leather is used to see clients on Sunday. Sometimes both Saturdays and Sundays for 2 years.

When Leather is migrating overseas these followers say to Leather it is time for them to retire as Tense's case is over. But the followers also migrate to the same place as Tense. Once Tense mentioned this to Leather. Leather pretends to be happy with a laughing face. Also Leather discloses, may be targeted at Tense, Leather wants to go to Cooden instead of Aooae. By this Leather means it is Tense's wish to go to Cooden. Actually it is for Leather's own advantages because many famous people go to Cooden. Leather also said it is Lance who advises him not to. Simply there is too hot and a big desert in the country.

Regarding Leather. When Leather is still a wealthy son. He is suspended by his uncle Less in the family company. At this time Leather has no money. Every month Leather has to ask Laws to give Leather money to support Leather's family. At later time when Leather recalls this incident. Leather says this period is no good. It is shameful to take money from his father every month. Is it true? Only Leather knows! Ask him yourself. Leather is a lazy man never does any work. Is it a shame? Only sit there and eat. He says it is a shame. Do you trust this big liar?

Then Leather borrows money from the family company to partner a business to manufacture children's toys with Leather's evil friend who has some nasty relationship with Terri's mother. Not adultery but this man, Mr Balloon, always pretends to be their uncle and visit Terri's mother Tane very often.

In the partnership the toys are very backward in style with small boats without any mortar to move the boat. Not up-to-date products. Terri's brothers tease it is rubbish. Then Balloon suggests to manufacture something smart and easy for sale. Leather may say nothing. Who knows? He never mentions this in front of the family members. Later on the partnership is collapsed.

Later on Leather still used to think he is great and rich. Whenever Leather is angry and find someone to express his anger. He says loudly that Balloon cheated him 3 times. Every time Balloon decreased $5,000 in the pay back because Leather withdrew from the partnership and sold back the shares to Balloon. Leather implies Balloon is a cheater and not to be trusted. Leather screams this matter more than 4 times before relatives and friends. After Leather's withdrawal Balloon's business returned to profits.

Later on Tense says that why Balloon did this is to cheat Leather's money. Leather dares not to mention this matter again. Why? Leather always tells any people he is great with talented characters and everything Leather does is correct and successful. If Leather again shouting on this matter. Leather will have no face and cannot command his siblings as he is not cute enough to be a commander. Good on you, man!

Another way Leather uses to test people are to let those people who will be following him to praise him as a great man then Leather is sure to give some benefits to that person. Then he brings the person to some social gatherings. Such as to dinner with Leather's siblings in a high class restaurant or anywhere that can show Leather's influences and rich. Then Leather will be walking around listening to that person's conversation with other people to see what he is talking about.

An example is Leather listens to his brother Little's words. At that time Little was appointed the Director of Family business. Little loudly said,"Inside the company which I worked. Senior management is trying to promote a staff in the section I am working. The man competitor is the Boss's friend or relative. That means they have some connections. It is sure to promote that person to a higher position but not me." At that time Tense does not understand why Little said this. Stupid Tense!

Tense has been in these occasions for a few times. When Tense was young. Tense thought to be a boss was good. At later life may be after seeing the family members' behaviour. Tense thinks if Tense is a professional. Even to be a boss in family business is no good. If you graduated and join the workforce. You implement what you have learned to apply in your job. Or maybe it is said to give back to the society. Then may be promoted or you have ability to set up your own business. Why bother to hide in the family business? It is stupid and ugly and shows your inability and incapability!

Another suffering to Tense.

While Tense is cheated to work in LL a company owned by Leather. The office boy eyes and shows his face to Tense 3 or 4 times. Why this office boy Cha has courage to do all these? It is most probably on Leather's consent. Why an office boy is brave enough to eye at Tense?

Every time when this happens then on the very same night Leather is used to dine with clients and leave office early. Every time it is the day that there are some goods from other retailer shops to deliver to LL. Also at this instance Cha has plenty opportunities to eye at Tense. Why Leather does it? There is a possibility that Leather wants Tense to do something to make Tense himself famous or Leather expresses his anger to Tense as no other person is best suited to be blamed on. Such as become an advocate on equal pay between men and women workers in Tense's living place. To lobby the government not to increase the bus fare each year. To demonstrate any citizen's grievances on social inequality or not to downgrade the education system.

While Tense is doing these. Tense is famous in the region and Leather has face as he is Tense's father. Not to mention other things but when Leather is walking on the streets Leather is identified by fellow civilians and all respect him such that Leather is the uncrowned king. Why not?

There is an evidence to prove this discipline of Leather's conspiracy and why Cha is dare to eye at Tense. One morning Tense starts to exercise Martial Arts at home only by himself. From then on Tense becomes more energetic and more cheerful. At this interval Tense is not planning to become any master or have some outstanding performances to show the world. Thus, Tense only practise on his own and that's it. Meanwhile Leather is very anxious to let Tense to become a master. Then it is the right time to tell Tense to work hard on Martial Arts. But Tense does not exercise too much. Then there is an occasion that a delivery of commodities to LL. As usual Cha shows his face. Tense is very annoyed and later calm down. There is a man Mr O watches Tense's response and think that Tense is willing to exercise. Does Tense have to behave so badly similar to a slave that after a humiliation then turns out to be a good boy to do anything that is told? Tense does not do much exercise after this planned insult! Alternatively why Tense has to do as told since Tense has no ambition on martial arts career!

Why Leather wants Tense to become a master? As stated earlier Leather wants Tense to become disabled. There may be a man/woman knows some other types of Martial Arts who comes up to ask for a fight. If Tense loses in the fight. Tense will either have broken arms and legs or a damaged kidney, liver or become a patient with brain injuries. This is what Leather wants. Leather can pretend to be a good father to look for anyone or anything to save Tense. Leather is going to do this without grievances. Does he have or not have? Whenever Tense is in trouble. It is a very good pretext not to bring Terri and Tense to migrate overseas together with Leather and Lance. Then Leather and Lance are able to speak loudly that they are correct and both are good husband and good brother to look after Terri and Tense until their migration. Again a good pretext not to migrate with Terri and Tense simply they are sick and disabled people. They are patients! Almighty God!

From this event it is crystal clear that it is absolutely to be sure Cha is under the secret consent of Leather to eye at Tense. The most important thing is to destroy Tense. From both Leather and Cha's viewpoint. Absolutely crystal clear and understood. Jesus why don't you come back earlier to save the sufferers?

One more. One day the goods need to be delivered to airport to be transported overseas. When the courier comes. Cha is still writing slowly to let the deliverers to wait. Also to show Tense that Cha is the person who has power and control Tense. If Tense does not listen to Cha. Tense is sure to be assaulted. On that evening Tense is going to Martial Arts class. Before Tense leaves the office Tense says to Cha that why Cha still wrote the documents slowly such that the deliverers had to wait a long time? Then Tense leaves the office to practise in Martial Arts class.

Leather has already told the staff he is going out with clients. When Tense comes back from class. Leather is already home having his dinner. As soon as Tense walks into the unit Leather asks Tense why he said such things to Cha. Leather's mood is to say Tense was talking nor cursed nor quarrelled nor scolded Cha. Before coming back home Tense already told himself that Leather is going to say all these. While Tense also told himself that why an office boy can eye at Tense and Tense is not able to curse the staff as Tense is the son of the boss. As soon as Leather has said all those words. Leather wants to continue the argument. Suddenly Leather realises Cha did eye at Tense before. Then quickly stops.

Is this all planned beforehand? Is he a good father or a hypocrite? A good husband and does not respect parents-in-law. Is this what Leather should do? Tell me!

One more strong evidence is there happen once. At that time the company LL is loading goods on a ship ready to sail to a client. Tense is told to stand there to watch that all goods are securely staying on the street without anyone stealing them and waiting to be boarded on ship ready to go. At this time Tense is very happy. Suddenly the office boy Cha eyes at Tense and saying something to insult Tense which Cha understands those words will definitely make Tense to become annoyed. Tense is very annoyed really. Suddenly Leather is standing at the back and moves Tense to the side of the street. It means to let Cha to insult you. Let him do it. Is Leather a good father to protect his biological son away from hazards? Leather tries hard to keep his son happy. Does Leather do all these are to make Tense happy? Or simply to express Leather's anger to Tense as Tense does not follow what Leather does in those criminal offences and evil transactions?

Are these all planned by Leather? Are these all to humiliate Tense? All the people at that time know Tense's situation know this plot but they never utter a single word. Those followers become good friends with Tense at later time is all because Tense has the super-natural feeling. Otherwise no one is going to help Tense. What they are saying at later time is to compare to the leaders in this world that Tense has got misfortunes happened on himself. It is because of all these sufferings that Tense realises the pities that sufferers conceive. Thus, Tense is good to those sufferers and apply good policy to help those needed. These are all lies, aren't they?

At this stage they all praise Tense has bad experience and hence, is going to help those sufferers and praise Tense is good and to compare to those famous leaders as to uphold Tense to a superior position. While Tense is suffering who is willing to come forward to say something in order to help Tense or to object Leather's cunny plots to humiliate Tense? They all feel very happy and always smiling especially when this plan is in action! The aim is to humiliate Tense as to express their anger whenever those people are shouted or scolded by their boss on their wrong doing of their work. Then pretend to be good people to help Tense. Every time after annoyances Tense returns to normal. These people always say good words as they are testing Tense's characters and always talking to Tense happily. Tense is in wonder. Why Tense quarrels with these people and afterwards they are not annoyed but still and always to show a happy face to Tense? Stupid Tense!

They are hypocrites! They hate you and treated you as a slave for them to express their anger whenever they are in trouble, man! Then tell you as pretexts that they are testing your characters and they try to identify you are a good or bad leader in the future. They say they are satisfied on what you are doing from these tests. They are able to not worry from these tests results. All ugly pretexts! After quarrelling are you able to talk to the person in happy mood and never recall the quarrelling incident which you have no excuses to tell yourself you should be friend with him again without grievances and retaliations? All they do is to play you as a doll as to move you anywhere they can upon their pleasure. When they are happy they will say 'Hello' to you. But while they are annoyed they look for any pretexts to harm you and then tell you these are tests, man! Stupid man!

Also from then on or started long before. Whenever they humiliate Tense and Tense turns to a bad mood as stated. They all say these are tests to certify Tense is a good boy. They insulted Tense and then telling all people in the world these are tests to verify Tense is good-hearted and a boy of good characters? That means they are bad-hearted because they plan such cruel tests as to insult and assault Tense to identify Tense's characters! Are these universal truths? Why only or always use humiliations? No other methods? How about I insult you to see you are a good person or not? After the assault I say to you that you are good. What is your feelings then, man?

At this time the only person who can help Tense is Terri. But these bad followers never ever utter a single word to Terri. Simply not let Terri to come to rescue Tense. By this Tense is isolated and secluded and no help from outside. Also Tense cannot do anything. Only suffer the humiliations and without retaliations. They all laugh and talk happily seems nothing has happened!

This is the only aid from outside. This is why Tense has got the super-natural feeling. This is what Fairy has helped Tense. This is to let Tense to revenge. This is to let Tense to realise there are ugly and ill-hearted people living in this world whom can do anything to destroy this world. All they are doing is to cause troubles and turmoils and to devastate peace on this world. Look at Kwok. He used to say in prayer to God --- "Peace on this world and peace in the hearts of people". But what Kwok is actually doing? He does everything that are opposed by our Almighty God's teachings! God is coming to make the peace in this world, man! You are certain to be penalised, man! See who is more powerful, man! Wait and watch, man!

In the court room,

"Mr. Leather, your two sisters tell you to leave the family house and you did not. Are you still in good relation with them?"

"Not with them but my father."

"Your son Ac says he saw you quarrel with these two sisters on the family meeting which is to discuss the arrangements of your father's fortunes. Is it correct?"

"Yes, absolutely."

"Then when you are trying to migrate to another country. As soon as your application is approved you tell your wife once you are there you will be good to your two sisters again. Is that correct?"

"Yes."

"Why at first is bad and later becomes good?"

"We are from the same parents."

"Then you do not care what they have done to your wife?"

"She is my wife. She is having a different last name with me. My sisters are sharing the same surname and from the same parents."

"Oh! I see. Before your application you induce Tense to work in your company but never give him any job."

"Yes, he can do nothing."

"Why does he can do everything while you want to show other people he is no good?"

"He is having luck."

"The office boy even shouts and eyes him and you said nothing. You tell your wife the office boy is able to earn profits for you then you refuse to fire the office boy. Correct?"

"Yes. Tense is only always losing his temper and can do nothing good."

"One of your friends says you are always losing your temper easily simply because he looks at you to turn to bad mood when Tense is having lots of food while having lunch with you. Correct?"

"Yes."

"You are not bad tempered then?"

"Of course."

"Every time the office boy eyes Tense. On the very same night you are always dines with your clients. Never stay home for dinner. Right?"

"It is coincident!"

"Well, one evening Tense quarrelled with the office boy then goes to his martial arts training. When Tense is back home. You ask why Tense quarrel with the employee. Correct?"

"Yes."

"Why you say Tense is wording the employee not quarrel? Is that Tense is not deserved to be the boss but even assaulted by an office boy?"

".................."

"Mr. Leather when you are applying for migration. The first step you induce Tense to work in your own office. Then always stir up a quarrel with Tense. It is to show to other people Terri and Tense both are neurological patients and thus, useless and hopeless. Also it is the excuse to tell both of them they are not able to migration simply of their illness. Correct?"

"………………, Well, they both come with me."

"It is all because of Tense is having super-natural feelings that you call off your original plan. Correct?"

"……………………………"

"Before you migrate you want to be a good brother with those two sisters again. Correct?"

"…………………"

"It is because you already known your brother Little is in dispute with you wanting to become commander in the family and is having a power struggle with you. Correct?"

"……………"

"Your Honour, other questions will be asked at tomorrow's early court. For the time being I have no further questions."

"OK! Court resumed at 9:00am tomorrow."

Above is stated again before or later in this story.

There happens some time ago. In the consecutive 3 to 4 months. Laws always goes to family house from office after lunch on Sundays. Why? On Sunday afternoons Laws sits in the sitting room quietly. Just sitting there. His married daughters bring their children to the house to play. Both daughters want Laws will be fond of their children not Tense instead. The children play and play.

On one Sunday afternoon there is a man selling balloons on the street. Laws buys the balloons to his grandchildren. When Tense is choosing his balloon. Tense realises that balloon will leak its air out. Tense insists to buy this one. It is because Tense had the experience a few days ago. Someone bought this type of balloon to Tense. The air inside the balloon came out and the balloon became flat.

After the purchase Tense goes back to the house to play. After 10 or 40 minutes or so. Tense returns to the balloon only to find out it has already become flat. Tense picks another balloon. The owner of that balloon screams to his mother it belongs to him. But his mother tells him to keep quiet on this matter to just let it goes.

Laws expects to see this incident on deduction that if and only if Tense is a good son. It is because after Tense was born up to that time that is around 4 or 5 years of age. Every day and every night what Tense notices are the bad women and bad aunts and the great grand-mother saying nasty things on his mother Terri. Tense is trying to revenge.

Another incident that on those weeks the toilet is always blocked every day. Laws finds out angrily and with the gossips of those women. Laws is in bad temper. May be pretending to do it. One night the people are quarrelling and screaming outside in the sitting room. Tense goes to toilet. On his way back to his bedroom Laws shouts at Tense, "Who blocked the toilet?" And Tense replies, "I don't know." Then quickly walks inside the bedroom.

The toilet is blocked. It needs a plumber. It costs money. Laws is so angry. Together with the gossips saying it is done by Terri. From what Tense said Laws knows Tense is a good boy. Never betrays his mother under any circumstances.

One night while having dinner with only Laws, Tense and a daughter of Laws called Lia. During the dinner time three of them are busy on taking in food. Suddenly Tense recalls that he deduces another aunt is a bad woman and wants to tell Laws. Then Tense shouts, "Aunt Lend is no good." But Lia stops Tense immediately. Tense realises Laws wants a whole family to be united and have no quarrels. Tense stops yelling and continues to eat his dinner.

After this night Tense does not see Laws at least for 2 or 3 months. One morning Tense and Lance go to the office. As soon as Tense steps inside the office. Laws rushes forward to murmur on the left ear of Tense. Then Tense is concentrated on the other people's talking. When the talking finishes. Tense walks to the sofa to sit down and rest. At this moment Tense recalls what he has heard just now. Then Tense deduces Laws is not a feudalist. At least not the same as what Leather always says Laws is useless and hopeless with totally all feudalist thoughts and ideas. But it is forgotten by Tense after that day's incidence. Only after many years Tense recalls this incident and tells his mother Terri.

One night, Monday night, Tense as usual watches TV programs till 11:30pm. While he is watching the series about a famous attorney general on his court cases. Leather suddenly comes out to the sitting room to watch television from his bedroom. The stories tell this attorney general is clever and clear the names of innocents. After this night's event Leather always argues and explains why Leather thinks Tense has to quarrel with his mother Terri. It is because Tense figures Terri is no good. This is absolutely rubbish on Leather's mind!

Tense is terribly hopeless. By this no one will listen to the explanations of Tense whenever Tense is trying to elaborate what Tense thinks and deduces. The aim of Leather is to provide a pretext to let people not to trust Tense no matter what Tense says. By doing this whenever Leather's bad conducts or offences are known to other people. No one believes in Tense and what Tense says are rubbish. This dirty trick is always used by Leather in the later life of Leather towards Tense. It also clarifies why Leather hinders Tense to study Law Course.

On Terri's behalf it is the ugly women always curse Terri that causes Terri becomes a neurological patient. Terri and her mother and brothers and sisters are very annoyed. All of them want a revenge. Why Tense quarrels with Terri? It's because Tense at first instance does not recognise the miserable life of Terri in her first 15 years of marriage. At first Tense is wrong. Later on, Tense comprehends this sad past. Tense always stands behind Terri and this marks the beginning of a long battle between Tense and Leather and the family members of Leather in later years.

"An eye for an eye. A tooth for a tooth."

This is what happened before Tense is admitted to hospital. Besides these Tense is feeling regret and sorry for the first error he makes in his long bad relation with Leather simply because Leather always using body language and gestures to mislead Tense to fulfil what Leather wants the outcomes to appear. Tense uses his influence to hinder Tah, son of Terri's sister Tar, to study in St Joseph same as Tense.

Upon these events can anyone suggests what life is Tense possessing along these years. An Emperor's livelihood or a dog's life? Superficially, it seems an Emperor's usual daily routines. Actually it is worse than a slave. Tense can still maintain his good characters inherited from his mother. Meanwhile Terri still is a pure and a considerate loving mother to Tense. Both of them are really good mother and good son.

On the contrary, people may say they are stupid. Simply because only people committing offences will become a rich person. Those good gentlemen and ladies are tended to become beggars. Is this axiom correct?

Terri and Tense both have a miserable life before the death of Leather. But many and many people say it is their journey in their lives. Should they or are they deserved such depressions for such a long time? No one knows! Or no one can affirm! In the near future or still years to come they actually still need to suffer? People say "God is a fair Judge. Good is rewarded while bad is punished." What is the time periods to wait on such happy days to come? How long or how many years to come?

Look at Terri and Tense they both never ever commit wrong doings. Never lust for money or power. In their surroundings are those mean people that do every single harmful trick to accomplish their goal of more reputations, power and money. Terri and Tense both still under pure character scenario, no crimes. Whenever other people try to induce them to the wrong sides. They think in another interpretation that convince them it is just a funny silly joke, it is fun or it is not true to tell them commit crimes. Are they both pure persons in this material and ugly world? May be it is really God's message to let them live. To spread human purity instead of crimes all over the planet before Christ's return! May be not! "Live and let dies". Honestly! Who knows?

After Terri married Leather. Terri does all work on her own. Later the family hired a servant in cooking and housework but Terri is already in bad health after two surgeries of her two babies. Her second baby is still alive with serious health issues only minutes after he was born.

When discharged from hospital Terri has to work immediately again from morning till night. Terri tells Tense once Leather told Terri that when Laws wakes up in the morning in the family house. Let Laws has his breakfast while Terri should stand behind Laws until he finishes his meal. At that time Terri can enjoy her breakfast happily afterwards. What an ugly rubbish!

In the first period of Terri's marriage. Leather goes out with Terri but Terri only to find out Leather always scolds Terri not calling the elders, not taking care of his brothers and sisters or Terri always done something wrong that stirs up a quarrel or dispute. Who stirs up a dispute? Why should call the elders first? What are they doing to me and my son? All you do is to please your father to let you to have a larger share of his fortune! Silly stupidity!

At first few years after the marriage sometimes Leather brings Terri and sisters of Leather to lunch or dinner. After the meal his sister tells Terri close to her ear secretly and quietly when they are back home. She says, "I went out to have a meal with brother actually is not what I want. I only pretended to be happy and enjoyed the food. I never ever feel happy with his physical nor spiritual presence."

Why the brothers and sisters of Leather so hate their brother Leather. It is a long story. When the children were young. Their mother's favourite son was Leather. She gave Leather all the powers to manage the house affairs. Bought food, went to picnic, what time to cook the meals and who was responsible for which housework.

At this time of the year Leather was like a King to do whatsoever he wanted. If the siblings did not obey his commands. Their mother would beat them. The children were very scare because they were still young without any help from outside and they were not strong enough to fight with their mother. Fortunately, Leather did all he can to give commands and expected absolute obedience. His brothers and sisters were very angry but what could they do?

After some years their mother was sick. It was a fatal disease. Her husband and mother-in-law always delayed her to make an appointment with a doctor on pretext that the doctor was a man while she was a lady. As far as Tense knows the delay took a long time which ended up her death because it was too late to be cured. Of course, Leather lost all power and as his usual trick always asks for helps from brothers and sisters on excuses they are siblings in the same family to re-gain Leather's influences and a good brother to them all. A dog. This is why Leather is so hateful by his siblings and father and grandmother.

Why Laws delayed his wife to see a doctor. It is all because of her conduct. She allowed Leather to do anything in the home. No matter how bad they were. This definitely arouses resents and disagreements among the children. It is most likely ends up in turmoils among the children that leads to not say "hello" in the future even coming face to face on a road or any circumstances.

After their marriage Leather lies to Terri that he was the beloved son of his father. After the marriage it is all because of the faults of Terri which annoys Laws and he turns away from Leather. These are all beautiful lies. Leather can show all his resentments towards Terri who does not call elders. If Terri calls elders Leather will have in a stronger position to show his obedience to Laws. Again Terri will have to do all the work whatever she is told. All these create a good enforcement for Leather to restore his influences and power. What is he doing? Does he love Terri or lusts for power? Leather even does not utter a single word of what he has done in the office during the day. To conceive the wife is this a good conduct or to hide his hypocrites and pretends to be a good man and husband? Ask God yourself, man!

Can someone give feedbacks to clarify this situation and recommend his way of doing is good or bad? Alternatively, give us information on what tactics to tackle his conducts. Is he conscience in doing everything he does? Sometime later in the life of Leather who is teased as "a man of no conscience". But Leather does the same, as usual, not utter a single word. Looks calm and not angry and still sits there just like nothing has happened.

When Leather is home he never ever tells Terri what he was doing on that day. He says it is like gossip in the market. Is he good? Why he dares not to say? Something wrong? Or these are ugly misbehaviours that do not deserved to be talked in public?

It is because Terri has a hard life at the beginning of her marriage. At the mean time Tense starts his study. Terri teaches her son to read and write in the kindergarten level. But fortunately Tense does not understand and Terri always scolds him. On one day Terri's friend living upstairs in an unit walks by. She tells Terri that to force a 3 years old boy to remember the whole chapter and learns to write properly is a waste of time and Tense is not able to cope with it. It is why Terri lets Tense to study instead of forcing him on those work that Tense is not able to cope with.

Terri's idea is correct. She wants her son to be brilliant. She and Leather send their son to a famous school to let their son becomes an useful not hopeless person. The idea is correct for Terri since Terri is always despised by her virtual husband's family members. On the behalf of Tense that it is because he is always to work hard and he scores a good mark. Tense never ever knows the reason that government set down policy to ask all children to study in school by laying down legislations to tell and then force parents to send their children to school.

On the behalf of Leather it is his desire to become great, to command the world and to dictate this world and his family that he forces Tense to study in famous school.

Leather always tells his son to study geography because at that time geologists earn a big income. Leather never tells his son he will be wealthy once he is a geologist. Then Leather has face and reputation inside and outside of the family. No matter what Leather does during in his life time. It is always for his own good and benefits. No other reasons to be deduced of, honestly!

The theory behind that to study in good college in order to obtain better education and brilliant student then goes to university and become a well-reputed professional is quite alright. This theory calculates upon the children's characters and what they are thinking and also about their conscience.

To receive good education is good for anybody. The teachers' quality needs to be also good. Otherwise a bad teacher educates students to the wrong path. There is an education student saying some college teachers they only teach not educate. The teachers go to college every day to teach their classes. Meanwhile the teachers tell students what they have just taught is not questioned in final examination paper. No need to worry. Is that true? God knows!

Whenever unfortunately there appears a good quality teacher and luckily he/she comes forwards with a smart student with a possibility to be famous in his/her future. What can the teacher do? The teacher can only teach or better to say to educate but nothing else. All is needed is the conscience in the students' heart and mind not to conduct evil matters!

Whenever the student is a bad-hearted child. Meanwhile fortunately the child has a good quality on study and the teacher is willing to give this child lessons. What can the teacher do? The teacher can only educate and nothing else. Is it true? There are examples!

Eva finds out later in her life that her boyfriend Adolf is a person lusts for power. Eva does not hinder his attitude and desire. Ironically, Eva lets him to do anything he wants. This causes millions of people lost their lives. A story book editor once draws pictures showing the path of a dictator's life from infancy to adulthood. When he/she is young. The dictator leads his siblings to fight other children or behaves badly in the family. While in college this person leads classmates to fight other school-mates. When the person becomes adult he leads his country to war. Is it correct? God knows!

It also happens in this way. Whenever you are a brilliant student and becomes first in classes every term. It does not mean you are a kind-hearted person. Look at this. If a girl becomes first in every term. It only shows she is clever but not anything. Why this girl studies hard? It may be she wants to marry a wealthy boy in implementing her university degree certificate as a bridge to marry into a famous family. Or after getting the required certificate she moves on to higher level. It only demonstrates her ability and intelligence not kind-hearted person. In the event she becomes a researcher she is still staying in her "lusts for power" stage and never get rid of it. Why she studies so hard? To marry a rich son to gain power? To become famous and influential? Ask God please!

It all depends on a person's conscience. A criminal breaks a law and sentenced to jail. When the gaol returns to society he continues to commit crimes and may be more serious criminal acts. If unfortunately, the gaol goes to chapel in prison to listen to the priest's teaching. The gaol may have a chance to repent. It can be witnessed in the later part of the story which Leather not to repent but instead still lusts for power and money to the day he dies.

On the contrary, if the spouse of a person has a same bad character as the spouse's spouse. Both of them is having a compromise to do not necessarily crimes but unethical conducts. Whenever your spouse is a good human being your spouse will persuade you to become good. If not or you continue to pretend to be good. It all ends up in a divorce if you are lucky. Others may end up in disasters. "God is fair to every person on this Earth."!

CHAPTER 5

At later life when Tense recalls. There are 3 incidents to prove Leather is a hypocrite.

On a night Tom invites Leather and the family to go out for dinner. As usual Tense does not attend. Then early next morning Tense is busy on something else with a happy mood in the lounge. Leather suddenly walks out of his bedroom into the lounge. Leather sees Tense and speaks, "This is not saying that you are great and on top of all other people." After hearing these Tense does not know why Leather said that. Does not know the purposes why Leather says these. At later life Tense realises Leather wants to follow Tom to say Tom is good. But whenever Tom invites to lunch or dinner. Tense refuses to go. By this Leather is very difficult to please Tom to say Tom is good. Hence, Leather wants Tense to go for the meals. Especially at that time Leather has no money nor influences. Leather wants to grab power and money. Thus, the only option is to follow Tom.

Another incident is Leather and Lance join together to conceal Tom. The father and son try hard to create opportunities to let Lance to chase Alice who is Tom's daughter the billionaire's daughter. But Alice refuses to talk to Lance. Both Leather and Lance are so angry that one night when they go home together. They quarrel on their way until arrive home. At that time Tense hears the quarrel but only one or two words and they stop. Tense knows there is something wrong. Also Tense understands it is only Tense can solve the problem. At this instance Tense still does not know what went wrong. Tense only observes there is something going wrong. Tense realises there is something wrong but actually does not know what went wrong.

The third incident is at that time Terri is having toothache and demands to see a dentist as soon as possible. The first available day is Wednesday. On this day Leather is asking all questions Leather wants to know from his evil friend Mr Fan on the racecourse, by which Leather knows he is no good but needs to use this man Leather thus says nothing but always goes to talk with Fan on the racecourse. By this Leather tells Tense to book an appointment on Thursday and not to let Terri knows. What is going on? What are you talking about? Terri is your wife for more than 40 years. Now you want to grab power, influences, money and reputation and just to leave your wife to suffer toothache one more day? Toothache is very painful but you don't care. She is your wife, man. She does housework every day and you Leather let her to suffer simply you want to grab power and leave Terri behind and also blame her is crazy? Is Terri your wife or alien? She is your spouse, isn't she, man? Where is your conscience? Are you a man or human or an animal? I say you are an ugly cunny animal that everyone will beat you and eat you up whenever people see you. Fairy has his penalty schedule. Take care! Watch out, animal!

Let's go back to the story. Why Tense studies hard? At first Tense does not work hard. Tense plays or hangs around whenever returns home from school. It is not until in class 4 which Tense one day or night suddenly tells himself to study hard. Then in that year he becomes the best student in class and is rewarded with a certificate. Even at this time Tense does not know why to study hard. He only knows that teachers always give assessments and tests is for the students to pass examinations not others. It is only when Tense watches the stories of the Attorney General that his wish is to become an Attorney. This desire stays there for many years in Tense's mind.

It is not until in the second 30- year series of the life of Tense that he wants to decide what career he is going to become. He loves thinking and dreams to become a cosmologist at the end period of his first 30- year series of life. At that period of time it is impossible for him to do that. Simply because his subjects in college did not relate to cosmology. Tense studied Arts class not Science class. While in the second series of 30-years-episode, unfortunately, he goes to a career full of decisive and potential thoughts and includes cosmology in his study. He studies Law degree and Science degree. At this time Tense deduces he is not capable to study Medicine degree. Simply it takes a lot of time and Tense is very old, 50 years of age. Unfortunately, a few years later Tense has got an opportunity to study something related to Medicine study and he loves it. He is very happy to go on to complete the degree. "Yes" for sure!

When Tense is working hard on his college homework Terri is having problems. As soon as Terri gets married. All family members of Leather curse Terri. They are to revenge on Leather's dictatorship happened in their childhood. Other elders are hoping to please the grandmother to attain their solid status in the family to monitor other family members and to have the final say on all family affairs. A paternal aunt does it often because her husband has altogether 5 wives. It means this aunt has no place to stand in front of her husband and is teased by other people. Most scary is from her husband's family members who do not say anything in front of her but tease her at her back. God! This aunt has heart disease and cannot do normal walking on her own at her later life. God's penalty? God!

When this aunt's husband is having a second wife. This aunt always goes to the living place to trouble this concubine. But her eldest brother that is Laws tells her not to cause any trouble since her husband is a business man. Such that gives him some face in front of other people and let him no need to hurry home and hurry back office all the time. But instead this husband marries again and again. Jesus Christ, how are you?

Since these bitches always gossip about Terri and Terri can do nothing. After more than 10 years Terri is diagnosed as a neuro-patient and admitted to hospital for one year.

During her time in hospital the sister of Leather that is Lie once asks her brother to bring her to see Terri. Leather refuses. Why? Leather is afraid of his father and Lie might cause more problems that annoys his father.

On the contrary, why Lie wants to see Tense in the hospital? This is the best trick Lie always performs. Lie wants to see Tense is really in hospital and is very sick then Lie can secretly and quietly curse Tense in front of any person especially Terri's relatives who at that time all are poor people. By this Terri's relatives can only listen to the curse but do nothing. Another trick is Lie will cry loudly and seems repenting to let all other people feel she is sorry and never bring up this matter again.

This is the usual trick she performs. In the event of an important person dies, such as Little's son who died in a house fire. Lie cries and cries loudly with her daughters in front of other people to show their sadness. It happens later in her life again. It is stated above when the younger brother of Lie that is Little that at that time his eldest son is dead. Lie and her daughter cry so loud it looks like earthquakes and volcanoes eruptions. After this scenario Lie and her daughter Boa return to the future. Again lust for money and power and harm any person whom they want to get rid of.

This family in this story is a mean family the Lung family. All descents are snakes. All want to occupy their father's money as much as possible. After Laws dies. One night in the family meeting Lie tells other members her husband is going to broke. It is why Lie wants a larger share of the fortune.

Regarding Lie when her husband is a rich man. Her husband beats her whenever he is angry. At that time Lie says nothing and continues to be beaten. After 20 years her husband has sold all his properties and Lie quarrels with him from time to time. Lie used to tell her family members her husband does not work in an office. A lazy man.

One day her husband beats Lie again. Lie says to other people Lie is going to divorce her husband. Why? Because her husband is a poor man now. Lie needs money to show off. Lie always shows her face to others. Now her husband goes broke it means she has no face. Then does it once and for all ---- divorce.

At this time of year Lie and Leather always try to persuade Tense to chase Lie's daughter Boa. But Tense always refuses. Why? It is their ugly tricks to Terri in Terri's first marriage episode. Once while Tense is standing at a bus stop waiting for the bus. At that time Tense is feeling dizziness. Lie drives a car pass by. In the car sits another worker relative Kom. Kom is told by Lie, most probably or most certainly, to ask Tense to travel home in her car. Tense knows it is Lie who drives the car. Thus, Tense refuses. Why bother to go back home in her car? Please tell me why, God!

All these family members are good at the art of cheating. Perfect! From this story whenever there is a person who wants to be a good person. This is an example to let them to copy not to learn absolutely from this story, not this way of doing your daily routines. Otherwise you are walking the same path as theirs. Finally, you are in deep trouble!

Also from this family we try to figure what evils do in their lifetime? They do evil things, of course! The question is "how evil"? These faceless affairs are what Laws is expecting. Laws has nothing to do but only goes to death and never sees his children again. Not anymore!

God is fair to all people! At first Lin and Lie always curse Terri is not pretty, not educated and not do anything correct. In the later life of these 2 bitches their daughters-in-law is short. The daughters in the family has no boys to date. These two bitches have no good food to eat. These two bitches always rely on the helps of other family members. Always beg people to give them mercy. God save the Queen! God!

God, when do you come back, please be quick! The true God or the Trinity has done his job. Has demonstrated his hatred to evils. God is still waiting to see you on Last Judgement Day. Come to join the club!

Honestly there is not many people have this mercy. Only on God's mercy. People used to say he is good. This is only to show their ugly face. It is because the person is a beloved son in the family. Nothing serious! Those people who tell their friends that they hate evils is only can be learned from fancy stories. Alternatively, you can find them in the World History if you are lucky. Good luck! No matter what it is true that you cannot choose your family. Nor the people you meet in your life. God! What can we do then? Can we do anything? It is from the movie, "Somebody do something!" Jesus! Alternatively, we can divorce our family, can't we? We also are able to divorce evil friends not to bother us any more for good!

No matter what after the case in hospital Terri and her maternal family members are so annoyed that they plan a revenge. At this point of time because Tense does not know the origins and reasons on this affair and the sufferings of Terri. At this episode Tense is not happy whenever Terri stirs up quarrels in the family. At later time when Tense knows the whole story Tense stands on the side of Terri. Nothing funny! Honestly!

No matter what after the discharge of Terri from hospital. After Tense scores the 4th position in class. After the death of Laws. It is the time for the down turn of Laws's whole family. It is all because of the family members of Laws, that is Laws's brothers and their family members. It really is God's power. God knows everything and God does show good to good people! Bad people are penalised by Almighty God! Leather and his brothers and sisters are thrown out of the family business because Less eats up the shares and swallows the whole company for Less to occupy and administered by his own. During this time episode Relau always tells stories of those businessmen who ate up other shareholders shares in the company. Then these people all ended up in bankruptcy. 20 or 30 years later it really happens. Less and all his family members all go broke and to work like a slave to earn their livings. God! You are so lovely, God!

In the suffering periods of Terri where is Leather? Leather is as usual, going to work early in the mornings. Goes out for dinner with friends, clients or sometimes with his own family. While Leather is at home. After dinner, as usual, talks to his brothers and sisters. Always and always Leather defames the brothers and sisters of Terri. Saying that her siblings are naughty boys and naughty girls. Always telling lies and lust for money or always show off in front of other family members.

Meanwhile Leather always says his siblings are good. When they were young Leather helped his mother to raise them up thus, Leather knows they are good boys and good girls. Are you serious? Are you kidding me? Who are good and who are bad, Mr Leather? Leather re-states and insists to inform his son Tense the same explanation. At later life of Tense, he realises all these faults and refuses to listen and firmly stands at the back of Terri and helps Terri to revenge, she is his biological mother! Look at those 2 bitches Lie and Lin. They only accuse Terri this and that but what happens later on? They accuse Terri is short and not beautiful. After 20 years their daughters have no marriage. Their sons' wives are short that whenever they catch a bus. Their feet do not touch the floor of the bus while they are sitting on the bus. This is God's punishments! God is good to Terri and always is! You devils!

Only a few years before Leather dies. Leather still tricks Tense several times wanting to punish and gives Tense an ultimatum. The tricks are to trap Tense into the status of a renal patient and together asks the neuro-therapist not to give medications to Tense for his illness. Once or several times Leather tries to set down a trap to let his 3 sisters to scold Tense whom at that time has no friends to come to his aid. Then force Tense to betray Terri and turns to the Lung family. Also tells and seduces and forces Tense to do things that are illegal and rubbish.

These scenarios are what Leather is telling Tense such as "if you go out and somebody gives you a lift. You need to say 'Yes' quickly and get on the car." Why should Tense say 'hello' to them? Whenever Tense asks a lift to supermarket. The driver family member complains Tense does shopping for more than 1 hour which is too long. Afterwards, Tense goes to shopping himself. That driver says politely to invite Tense to give Tense a lift. Real bastard!

Why Tense asks for a lift? It is because at that time Tense supposes the family members are good to Terri and Tense. On the contrary, they join together to do every dirty trick to harm both Terri and Tense. These murderers include Lance.

Leather's family members set a pitfall to tell Terri secretly without Tense's presence. Saying that Tense is not capable to do all the work. Tense is a sick person and only knows to lose temper whenever he is able to. Whenever Tense is annoyed Tense threatens to leave Terri such that Terri will be living alone. Especially Lance threatens Terri he will never ever to buy food or visit Terri if Terri sold the house. Inhuman!

When Leather is going to die all other members want him to die as soon as possible. It is because after Leather's death Tense has to kneel down to beg them. When this moment comes they are in a superior status and most importantly they have already got rid of Leather. They can do whatever they want to do. Especially they want to humiliate and tease Terri and Tense either privately or publicly. Their expectations are all wrong. It is then they are in turmoil! Simply Tense stands firm to protect Terri and Tense himself! Simple as that! God!

Once Lance recommends to hire an electrician to install air conditioners in Terri's house. The air conditioner is extremely cold in the room of Terri. In the room of Tense it is not strong and the temperature inside the room is always over 26 or 27 degrees Celsius. God is doing his job! A year later that electrician company closes down.

Leather creates many occasions to trap Tense to stay in a tolerable condition in respect to Lance's bad temper. Once and happen many times on the excuse Lance is doing good things, buys food for Leather to eat but loses temper to quarrel with Leather. There is a misunderstanding at that time between Leather and Lance. Or it looks like a misunderstanding! Is it really? Not really!

In the wedding ceremony of Lance. The photographer cuts the part that shows Tense saying 'Hello' to Lance. This company also closes down in a year time. Why? In the future whenever watching this video Lance blames Tense not good to Lance and caused chaos in his wedding ceremony. It is because they have proof. Why? It is to tell Tense to tolerate Lance on no matter what Lance does or family members of Leather have done anything wrong. Tense needs to rush to help. If not, they show the video again and Tense is the white dog.

Another trick is at that time Tense is delivering bottled milk in his neighbourhood. As the illness is getting worse because of no correct medications prescribed from neuro-psychologist. Tense always feels worry whenever it is on the day of delivery. Once Tense rings to resign and will not take the wage for that week. Days later Leather says Tense is not dared to cheat the boss. Tense is coward! Look at this, it is illegal! Tense will go to jail. Tense dares not commit crime! It is you do the crimes and it is you who must take the responsibility!

All these dirty tricks failed! God is on good person's side! After the death of Leather his family members expect Terri and Tense will obey and follow their instructions. It is after 3 to 6 months they find out they are all wrong. Tense is determined to crush them. Once and for all! It only consumes time, man! Who is going to win, man?

Regarding Tense's first 6 months in company LL. It is worse than a dog! Leather stirs a quarrel every now and then. To send his followers to let Tense know Tense is in turmoil and needed to turn to Leather for help. Also not attending dinner party in order to let Tense to represent Leather instead. This is to show Leather's willingness to give the business to Tense. But indeed does it happen?

In this first 6 months Cha already eyes at Tense with Leather's silent or verbal consent. Leather as usual pretends nothing has happened before! The first girlfriend of Tense is also sacked by her company boss under Leather's influence and advice. Why? Simply the girl does not listen to Leather after marriage! Leather, the same trick of his uncle Less and this is cursed by Leather himself, is always to oblige any person to obey Leather. Not only listen to but to obey! It proves Leather must be on top of the world! Does he have this capability and ability? Fortunately, he has none! Or unfortunately?

After the dismissal of the girl Leather sets a trap to keep Tense in a pitiful situation and finally goes overseas to have a change of environment. But why? It is all because Terri's billionaire brother Tom invites the family to go on vacation. Leather is sending Lance to chase Alice who is Tom's only daughter. In order to succeed they must not let Alice has the impression that Lance's brother that is Tense is a patient. But not Terri! Why?

It is all because whenever Alice finds out Terri's situation Alice realises it is the dirty tricks of Leather's family and figures the family is no good. Then under Lance's impression to show Lance's genuine love to Alice then Alice is willing to marry Lance as Lance has already to demonstrate that he is good or pretends to be a good boy but not the family members. Indeed, Alice never ever talks to Lance. Later when Leather works out Alice is good to Tense. Leather creates many opportunities for Tense to see Alice. Tense's impression on Alice is she is arrogant and having dark skin. That is no good! They are not going to talk to each other since then! The conspiracy fails and also follows by which Leather dies! Who knows?

CHAPTER 6

Regarding Tense it is also no good! Tense is treated like a dog in Leather's own company LL. One Summer his brother Letton's family comes back from overseas for holidays. They visit LL to say hello to Leather. This incident is a tiny reflection of what Tense is suffering. Similar to Terri may be worse than Terri and worse than a dog!

Letton goes to the company with his family members. On first sight Tense observes there is something wrong. Later Tense listens to Letton's conversation with Leather's partner Lee. Tense knows he is correct! Then Tense invites Letton family to lunch. Leather realises Tense's intention is good and Tense is doing the right thing then Leather pretends to do the same thing. Leather brings Letton's 2 elder daughters to buy a gold watch for each of them.

One afternoon Letton's two younger sons stay in LL. They both help to do some work. They help a little bit actually! The commodity is finalised by handing to the office boy Cha to put into a big box. Once the two sons forget to put a plastic label on top of the small box. Cha turns his face and shows to Tense and Cha's face means Tense is no good, always done wrongs and not suitable for any job. Only Cha himself is the best and better than Tense. It is why Tense has to listen to Cha. Listen to your stupidity and foolish ideas, man?

After the holidays Letton family returns home. The first working day after Lettons's leave. Cha sits in his desk with a black face. It is because Tense is correct and Cha has lost a chance to tease and curse Tense. By this Tense will have confidence in his future life. Cha is sure to destroy it!

What Tense realises is Letton's two older daughters are not happy and hate Letton very much. Why? It is all because Letton always saying he does not know anything on history, geography or civics. Letton wants to encourage the two sisters to work hard on school assignments. But the two girls feel they are humiliated and is a shame to say they are worse than every other person in front of these people. When Letton family goes back home. They go out to lunch and dinner. Letton goes to gambling. The two girls are happy and restore their self-esteem. At later life one of the sisters Lzz is going to marry a rich boy. The Letton family shows their face to Terri and Tense. Lin has a baby daughter. Later on Tense finds out the baby is brought to every family of Letton's siblings but not Terri's.

What are they doing? They show off! The son-in-law is rich. Even on wedding party the Lettons plans to humiliate Tense in public that is in the restaurant premise. Tense sits in the restaurant with Terri without saying a single word not even have a photograph to be shot with the Letton family.

It is why the family not only Lettons but all are doing a revenge to Tense to force Tense to tell them anything which Tense has got from his supernatural feelings. Also uses the super-natural feeling to commit crimes for the advantages of Lung family. Only Tense does it. Whenever there is police it is Tense's business not Lung's business. The Lung family will walk away from jail free! Good trick which Leather is the master mind! Tense helped them in the past such as the example given above and now Tense is a gaol to be checked on in the family gatherings and whatever Tense does and Tense has to report to the family. Jesus why don't you come back earlier? Let us not to suffer too much burdens and live a better life from then on, please!

One morning Tense suddenly asks Leather to bring Tense to the retailer clients together with Leather to learn business techniques. Leather shows an ugly face. Then in the company Leather brings the office boy Cha to retailer clients to learn business. After a few weeks it is dropped. Simply Cha is so stupid that he is not able to learn and digest all materials from Leather. Even Leather repeats and repeats Cha is still having no clues. Leather has no options but turn to his brother's son Lan.

Frankly, all matters inside the company such as to look at the commodities which are good or bad. Leather never ever teaches Tense. Not even Lance. Why? Because when Leather was working in his father's business. It was Leather suggested to Laws he has to learn business. Otherwise Leather has no clue on the business after Laws's death. Laws hired a teacher for Leather then. After Leather has learned all the business skills Laws is obliged to retire from the company.

If Tense has learned all the business tactics Leather has to retire. This is not what Leather wants and expects. Thus, no teaching. Honestly, all the techniques Tense learned is by Tense's own observations and deductions. No one helps Tense ever! Ever!

When Terri is suffering Leather still goes out early in the mornings and comes home late at night. It is a pretext that Leather tells his friends he knows nothing from start to end of what Terri is struggling. Is it true? Are you kidding me? From the beginning you do not love your wife! All evil things are originated from you. Are you ashamed? You never ever feel this. It is because you have no conscience! You are worse than a snake, man!

The behaviours of Leather do not change from the second he was born up to the second he dies. What a bastard! Hurting people all his life without any repentances nor regrets. Behave yourself! That's why you have renal failure at the moment you were born! God is showing his strength and mercy to good and evil people, man!

Leather used to use this ideology to attain his power and money desires. His usual tricks are in order to stay on top of other people and he has to grab and hold tightly on what you have. That is power of any form to control you severely and to stay rich in having lots of money to the aids of accomplishing his ambitions. Also thus, you will have plenty of girls. To accomplish this. It is to suppress others to a position whom they will be without any money. Without counter-attack power and most importantly is without self-esteem and no self-actualisation. Simply to say it is a slave dog.

After his marriage he treats his wife Terri seems as a slave. As mentioned stand behind Laws when he is having his breakfast. This is what a servant maid is doing but is Terri a servant maid or daughter-in-law, man? After he finishes his breakfast Terri is allowed to eat her own breakfast. All Big Bastards!

Terri has no money in the first 10 years of her marriage. This means Terri cannot go out to have a cup of coffee nor have dinner with her sisters nor friends. Terri is always staying home to do housework from dawns to nights. Not even allowed to drive a motor car to bring children to school and back home on pretext that she is a patient. This is lie. Does Leather lie? Does Leather never lie as he is a gentleman? Ask God, mate! Don't bother to ask me, man!

Why it all looks like this? It is the strategies of Leather to stay on power and to stay on top of all other people. To suppress Terri as Terri is not educated and has no friends which means Terri has no social life. To keep her down and blue that everyone looks down upon her especially on her neurological disease. Every time Terri talks to someone either at home or going out. Then afterwards Leather definitely asks for the details. Then it is Leather's turn to decide how to punish and ruin the self-esteem of Terri. Leather does the same to Tense. Both of them are submissive thus, no quarrel, no disputes and ironically suppose Leather is a good person who is for the sake of them to let them live better. It is all because of Leather's arts of acting and to tell lies are at the top level than every other person in this world. Leather's skills to do evil thing is good enough to evade all types of punishments especially legal penalties but not from God's, man!

Every day in the office Leather phones home to check where is Terri or has she done her work. If Terri tells him she is going to go out. Leather phones many times back home to see how long Terri was out. If it is a long and very long periods of times, then Leather will show his face to Terri. Leather phones back home in front of other people on pretext that Leather wants to know where is Terri and is Terri back home already? Or has there any accident happened? Human Bastard!

Leather wants to cut off the relationships between Terri and her brothers and sisters. Whenever something happens Leather always lies to Terri saying that person involved is no good because that person did this and did that it is inhuman or not logical or insane complaining Tense that his thinking is totally irrational and full of nonsenses. At later life Tense argues with Leather by simply saying, "Your brothers and sisters are good people. Other people's brothers and sisters are bad people!" At that time Leather wants to argue over Tense. But before this Leather's siblings have shown their ugly faces to Leather. Meanwhile Tense notices these and even Leather says in front of his siblings that Little is lying to Leather on all family and business affairs at that time Tense is also present. Then Leather keeps very quiet! Bastard! God is coming, man! Bastard!

Leather will definitely also cut off the relationships of any person with Terri whom the person says to Terri what to resist or lobby her rights in the family. Leather simply to isolate Terri and that particular person to have no communications such that Terri needs to beg him on any matter as no friends turn up to Terri's aids.

These are all the strategies of Leather which his followers adopt his methods to ruin the life of Tense hand in hand with the family members of Leather including Lance after Leather's death later on.

It happens two times. Once Tense is telling Leather that Tense wants to do business with his friend. Leather without any knowledge of what they are discussing. Immediately says his friend is trying to cheat the money of Tense.

The second time Tense has bought some cosmetics ready to sell locally. As soon as Leather heard this news Leather immediately says Tense's money was cheated by someone else. Why Leather did this? There are 2 incidents.

The first time is when Tense is working in the office of Leather. In that period Tense was a dog even the office boy shows his face to Tense. On a day Tense asks Leather to give Tense a few thousands of dollars to buy stocks. Leather refuses and scolds Tense by saying to learn to do business only with 3 thousand dollars. After a while Tense takes out one thousand and a half to buy the shares from Tense's own pocket. After less than a year there is a profit of a little bit more than one thousand dollars.

As soon as Tense has sold his shares. Leather arranges a trap that leads Tense spends all his profits. By doing this Leather is able to complain Tense expends money extravagantly. It is no good. In reality, Leather tells the girlfriend of Tense to show Tense that his girlfriend has bought many watches, many bracelets and many sunglasses plus all other many things. From this Tense has to buy lots of things which means Tense is a big spender. Then Leather can blame Tense in expending all the money of Leather if Leather gives his business to Tense.

Another incident is that during that period many people are expecting the share market and property market bubbles are going to burst. Leather as usual lies to people saying after 5 years or so the economy is in disaster.

At this moment Tense expects the markets will rise again. Therefore, Tense buys a couple of shares from his compensation payment at the end of the year. Leather scolds Tense demanding to sell all shares as soon as possible. After Tense has done this Leather phones Tense for details and to insult Tense. Leather says on the phone, "Ah! Ah! You see."

Actually after less than 5 years the markets are at their peaks again. If Tense sells his shares at this moment. Tense will get a big profit. These are what Leather does not want to see because Leather is worse than Tense and his siblings will all support Tense. Also Tense is capable to do business and earns a big profit. Then Leather will lose power.

Meanwhile Tense always utters that he is honest and shows his good-hearted characters to all people Leather knows. Once Tense asks Leather to sell the shares for Tense. Leather on return to home tells Tense that the company has collapsed and is not in the share market of the country it used to be anymore. Before Tense's migration Tense understands the company's share is rising. Now suddenly it is out of business! God!

One more incident while Tense gets 1,000 dollars from Leather and let Leather to get back the money by exchanging to another currency when Leather is in the other country on this planet. Leather replies that the exchange rate is 1:6.85. But Tense understands that it is 1:6.20 around this rate. It means Leather fraudulently takes 700 dollars more into Leather's pocket.

Leather gives lots of money to Lance to spend without saying a word. Every time it is $500 and together with 2 houses as rental income. On the part of Tense he has no money. In the evenings before Tense is going to study Tense will have early dinner in restaurants which only costs 10 or 15 dollars each time. It is because Leather has promised to give the money back to Tense. At that time Leather shows his face to Tense while Tense is asking for the money without saying a word to imply Tense is a big spender. It is done! All tricks are the same to Terri and Tense. All are Hypocrites in the family!

Before the death of Laws Leather is the commander of his brothers and sisters. At this period Leather looks like Julies Cesar that everyone has to say "Yes" to what Leather said. Leather has no challenges and everything is decided by Leather and unopposed. But after the death of Laws everything is changed. Leather has no money and falls from power! Good stuff and good luck, Bastard! Every relative and every brother and sister is against Leather. By now Leather lives in the same life as a dog!

Another point is Leather always tells other people especially his brothers that leather is a businessman from onset. It means Leather is skilful in doing business and cautious at the tricks in business under table dealings.

While in racecourse a man called Shum, a house builder, also gambling there. Fortunately, they talk to each other. Leather introduces Shum to Leather's own brother Latie to renovate Latie's house. Suddenly Shum runs away together taking all the money Shum has. After Shum flee away Leather has no face! Leather says he is a businessman. Oh! My God! Are you putting penalties on evil people? God!

Leather works as the son of the boss in the company. At later life Leather has no money and intentionally teases his paternal uncle's son Bee by saying Bee used to call Leather whenever Bee saw Leather while Bee was studying in high school. Later on all other family relatives or family members or at least has some relationships with the Lung family. These boss's sons all earn big profits from various types of trade transactions in different businesses. Look at Leather. He is only a man in poverty and relies on the money that are cheated by himself from other family members! Is Leather a skilful businessman? Is Leather a liar? Does Leather commit any crimes? Please tell me honestly! God!

CHAPTER 7

When Tense is admitted to a new elementary school St Joseph it is seeming to watch a comedy. At that time Tense does not know what is happening inside the school and forgets everything that were told by teachers. The class-mistress tells the students to memorise the "Good Student Commandments". While Tense is home Tense forgets everything and only eats dinner then goes to sleep. The following day the class-mistress picks pupils to repeat the 10 Commandments. Tense at this moment realises he forgot. Unfortunately, he is not picked up by the teacher. Finally, the whole class is told to say the 10 Commandments all together. Tense only opens his mouth pretending he is doing the same job as others. Then another day comes it is happening all the same episodes. A repeat of history. When Tense is expelled from St Joseph at that time Tense still does not know the 10 Commandments. But only the last one. "To read as many dirty books as you can".

In the English class the teacher teaches the class to sing the song "A B C". Most of the other pupils already know the song but not Tense. Also the teacher only teaches the song for a few times and the song is very long. Tense forgets the last part of lyrics as it is difficult to memorise and Tense does not know the trick what to sing or why other students pick up quickly but not Tense. Fortunately, after expulsion Tense still does not know the lyrics of this song.

Also happens in the first year. There is a class period for pupils to practise handwriting. For the first 2 months Tense is usually to be in detention class to do the job again. The last time in detention class the class-mistress shouts at Tense this page of handwriting is very bad. On Tense's opinion it is actually very good.

Tense is told to write or re-do it. While doing the second piece of writing Tense's fingers suddenly move to the directions that should not be moved. Tense thinks it is omen. While handing in the copy of writing. The class-mistress Ms Savs says it is very good. Jesus, why don't you come back earlier? This is the last time in detention class. After this class Tense is allowed to go at the end of school each day.

Once it is recess time Tense walks out of the classroom happily. Suddenly a pupil is running towards Tense and they clash together. Tense lost his hearing instantly. Tense on second thought, tries to say something or tries to listen after 2 or 3 seconds. Then it is OK. At later life his ears are always having problems. Is this the reason? God knows!

First talk about Terri. At this time of the year it is the matured time to revenge. The two sons are growing older whom the elder son Tense is in puberty stage. He should be looking for girls. By this at every time Terri and her mother Tan go out or appear in front of Tense and Lance. There is something connected to girls.

One night the maternal grandmother is visiting Terri. She brings her with a girl not more than 14 years old sitting in the sitting room where both mother and daughter talking together. Lance at this time goes to bathroom to bathe. Lance walks out of the bedroom with a short pants and singing during his bath. Meanwhile Tense says nothing. Tense understands it is a pitfall thus, never talk to these girls. Honestly, at this time Tense is not keen on girls.

What Tense thinks and fancies is to be smart and intelligent to attract girls but not these types of girls. Actually, before the death of Laws Tense has already a few girl classmates to play with. Every day while in class the girls quietly take away his school bag, or textbook anything like these. Tense really is thinking of marrying one of the girls. But it is only a dream or fancy. Frankly, at this stage Tense does not have any desire to know girls but stays on study.

The girls play with Tense but Tense does not understand the reason why? Tense supposes it is his academic result to be 4th in class. Nothing else. The teacher an old lady realises the motive but only teases on the stupidity of Tense.

Also because of this Tense is defamed by the classmate Jik. He tells whosoever knows or have contact with Tense, that Tense is mean and does all ugly dirty things. This arouses the hatred from other classmates. Also is the beginning of the lonely life of Tense.

Before this incident Tense has phone calls from a girl in the same elementary school from time to time. Tense does not know what to talk. Every time it is the girl takes the first initiative. Once Tense asks the girl to ring again after the final examination. The girl says nothing then hang up. Never ring again. Tense foolishly takes this as a joke telling some of the classmates. As Tense later expects the girl is expelled by the principal for sure!

The revenge from Terri and her family members lasts not long only for around 9 years. In these 9 years there are always quarrels inside the family to produce no peace episodes. Terri is correct. Tense does not understand the feelings of Terri. Tense always quarrels with Terri at a later period. When Tense is attending a private University Tense wants to return to peace and talks happily with Terri.

Honestly, Laws understands what is happening. He is deducing and expecting it. But says nothing. It is all the faults of the Lung family members. True! At the first episode Tense goes to school every day. Lance does the same. Leather goes to office to work as an employee not the boss. Leather mentions to Terri that he quarrels with his uncle every day.

Because of the death of Laws the two grandchildren suddenly losses something. Lance turns to Tense, Leather and then to aunt Lisses for family love. All refuse him. The Lisses always scolds Lance and Lance has no place to turn and is forced to gamble with the boyfriend of Lisses whom later marries Lisses. Lance does it is to have someone to love him. The reality is Lance finds the wrong target. This incident is found out by Tense. At later life

Tense argues with Lisses saying she is harming both of them as soon as grandfather was dead. Lisses says she cannot recall. Tense tells her at one incident her sister is also attending the premises. Lisses says nothing and does all her usual tricks to pretend to feel regret and guilty. Then turns out to become a good person again. Her brothers believe in her especially Leather.

Why? Because Leather needs the help of Lisses to introduce business friends for both Leather and Lance to do business. Both of them tolerate Lisses's arrogance and ignore Tense. Leather goes to lunch with Lisses without taking Tense and even not mentions to Tense of the incident. They include Tense as director in the company but his job is to bring cheques to a bank and answers phone calls. That's it! Why? In doing this Tense is part of the company. Tense will pray to Fairies to prosperous the company. Leather has introduced a girl to Tense which means Tense must accept the position otherwise Tense cannot support his own family.

Secondly, Tense cannot go to study since he has to stay at home office 6 days a week. If Tense goes to night classes. Leather is sure to make Tense very fatigue on that day to disrupt Tense's learning. If Tense quarrels with anyone and says he is going to leave the company. Tense has no friends, no certificates and no money then he can do nothing.

One more there is an occasion that the Lung family has a property to earn rental income. In a general meeting in a year Leather tells his brother Little to nominate Tense as director in the family business for that year. Other members in the board of directors all object. Little is going to call Leather to report the whole lot. When Tense is home again. Tense rings to Leather who is on another country to tell Leather that even Tense is appointed as director. Tense refuses to accept. Why? Look at this family!

When Leather comes back home for 3 or 4 months after this occurrence. Leather arranges an occasion to let Tense realises his uncle Little is telling lies to Leather meaning turmoils are coming. This part of story will be saying that they are in a power struggle to be commander instead they are blooded brothers.

At that episode Terri is living under horror and revenge. Leather still forces Terri to do all housework by saying the 2 sons are still small. Not strong enough to help in the house work. Terri works days and nights. There is a period of 6 months that the whole family lives with Tom. Tom is the brother of Terri. The first few days moving in Terri intentionally breaks the wardrobe. Tom always finds excuses to insult Leather and Tense.

In a week night Tom has 2 friends visiting Tom. They talk for a long time and then have seafood. At that night Tense is having skin disease. Tom asks Tenses to eat repeatedly for several times and Tenses supposes it is a good will and eats a little bit. But His brother Lance blushes and says nothing. Tom insults Tenses. Why? In Tense's infancy Tense knows nothing about misconduct. Every night has dinner in maternal grandmother's home Tense used to say something about Tom. Frankly, after what Tense has said Tense does not know what he is talking about. But the words said is to mean Tom is no good. Only one night Tense's nephew Albert says the words are humiliating Tom that Tense commences to stop talking any more from then on.

One matter Tense regrets to Albert is Tense uses his influence, more details later, whom the principal gives Tense that he obstructs Albert's entry into the same college as Tense. At that time Tense is already a neuro-patient and Tense does not want this to spread out. In that period Leather is in dispute with Albert's mother. Leather one night intentionally rings to Albert's mother Tracy telling her the application is rejected.

Before this telephone conversation Leather again intentionally may not be face to face telling Tense that Albert is applying to his same college. Why Leather impliedly saying this to Tense? It is because before the conversation talk Leather already knows Tense has got approved influence from the principal Kwok. Leather may be not happy Albert's application which will destroy Tense and his brother Lance study in the college. May be at that time Leather has no influence in the family and office. Leather is used to be blamed by his uncle Lang that stirs up many quarrels.

It is Leather's idea to put the blame and his anger on Albert. Before this Leather is not happy with Tracy that she brings Terri and two sons to go out with Tracy's family. As Terri goes out the family is certain to dispute again and Leather is in a turmoil position which affects his power and influence both in family and family business.

Terri's horror still goes on and on for a long and a long time until the death of Leather. After the death of Leather's father Laws. The whole Leather family is living under the shadow of misery. Terri is having bad moods also because of her illness. Tense is having problems with his stomach. Lance is looking for help and love from those people that pretended to be good to him long time before when Lance was young. There is no smiling face in the family. Especially Tense because of the death of Laws.

Six months after Laws misfortunate death Tense is having a Sports Day in the college. At an instant Tense walks with another boy scout Tense sees a girl, Monster very beautiful and never takes his eyes off. Tense still watches Monster while doing his service in St. John Ambulance.

When the corporal tells Tense to stop watching. Tense does what he is doing just like nothing has happened. After a while the teacher responsible for the Ambulance section comes over to say something to corporal. It means to warn Tense to stop watching. Regarding to Tense's fool and Tense tells himself it is not for him. Tense keeps going. The teacher is sent by Kwok because Kwok strongly opposes loves between boys and girls in the college. Later Kwok crushes their affair and pretends only a minor merit to bring back Tense to study hard and never not to mention to pretend not hoping to be famous in this world.

After that Sports Day and followed by term examinations Tense works hard to pass. Then the start of second term. Before Easter Holiday Tense recalls the incident and try to figure how to chase Monster. Tense rings her a few times but hang up by her brother. Monster's father has 8 wives.

Then Tense thinks of following her back home after school. This method needs to take serious consideration. Before the final decision is made. One day after Tense's school day and Tense is walking after Monster. It makes the stupid Tense to follow her right back to her home. Tense is in love for the first time after the death of Laws.

This affair goes on for a few months and nobody knows. One day the class mistress tells the class to read a chapter then calls Tense to come outside of the classroom. The class mistress asks for details and demands him to stop. In that same afternoon before Monster walks inside her living place Tense asks for details. Monster says "Yes, I told the teacher."

Tense is very upset and thinks about this matter again and again after revision of Chemistry school notes at home. Finally decides to do the same thing. It is by this time Tense finds out other girl class mates of Monster report to the teachers. A boy once says to Tense before morning assembly, "Class one girls tell class two girls you follow Monster to her home and she has to smile to you then you say bye-bye!" Tense does not reply. Only afterwards figures out there is something wrong.

The affair continues for another 3 or 4 months that comes a mid-term holiday. At this time Tense thinks there is not much hope to succeed. Or the girl may not love him. Or other matters that are no good. Or something that he does not understand. Or perhaps they are not supposed to come together. Or maybe the girl is not good.

No matter what suddenly Tense receives a call from his best friend Gogo. They agree to go out for tea. At tea time another boy accompanies them. In the restaurant both watches the beautiful maid servant except the other boy. They go out 2 times but only watch other girls instead of talking or really discussing. Finally, Tense rings Gogo to discuss the matter and not going out in a restaurant.

Over the phone Gogo persuades Tense stops chasing Monster because they are both not fit. Gogo rang to Monster to talk with her. In the telephone conversation Gogo mentioned Tense's other name for several times but Monster asked him who is this boy? She even does not know anything about Tense.

At first Tense is thinking to quit. Upon this conversation Tense still cannot decide. When school resumes Tense go to study as usual. But still deciding. After school he sees the girl walking slowly. Tense realise many people know this affair and sees her walking so slow which she intends to or not to let Tense to follow her again. Tense doesn't know! Then Tense decides not to follow and the affair is over. Later on Monster's father sent her to study overseas and this is the end of the story or this affair! God!

After this Kwok wants to know why Tense stops this chasing because in the future Kwok can arrange a similar incident to stop any affair of Tense. The teacher tells the class to write a composition and return it the next day. Tense does not write down what happened. This matter is finished.

After this Kwok finds a chance to call Tense to the principal's office to talk with him. In the first part of the conversation Kwok says anything Kwok can think of that suits Tense characters not to show off but indeed he has already done it. She is a psychologist. Later in life Tense's father Leather uses the same trick but modified to the extreme best level to induce Tense to fall into his trap such that to expand Leather's influences and power.

Then they talk about Tense illness. Then the Principal says to Tense face to face, "If you find out anything you are not happy. Come straight to my office to tell me." Tense never ever uses this influence except on the case of Albert. Afterwards both quarrel to each other which leads to Tense's departure from college.

After this conversation Tense still study. But the sickness of Tense is going from worse to worst. Tense does not work hard simply if not working hard he can still be promoted. From then on Tense watches television every night. Finally, Tense is admitted to hospital.

In the occupational therapy of the hospital. The coach of wood work treats Tense very good. He, master You, always talks to Tense at that time while Tense is recovering. You gives Tense many jobs to be leader and directs the group members to work or play football or playing bingo. Always, some of the patients are not happy and Tense knows that. But You always does it. It is later on, may be accidentally or You realises the outcome and then ceases.

After his discharge Tense is involved in another affair which leads to quarrel with Kwok and then expelled from college. Then also starts the other episode of Tense in his life which is even worse and much bitter.

CHAPTER 8

Let's talk about Leather. Leather as stated has a partnership company with his maternal uncle Ching. In this company there are another 2 more partners. One is Ching's biological son Chit. The other is Leather's relative or as said that he is Leather's cousin Lez. Both Chit and Lez have 5% share each in the company. While Leather's got 20% and Ching is the big boss who owns 70% of shares.

In the first 2 years of operation the company goes on the right track and got profits every year. During this period Leather always suggests good advices to Ching in order to manage the company in the right direction to more profits. Ching is very happy and thinks Leather is a good boy who really needs Ching's help after Leather's expulsion from his family business after the death of Laws.

But all things are not going smoothly as expected and hoped. On one occasion Chit's friend visits the company. Leather uses this opportunity to ask Mr Oo to play basketball somewhere else where they need to travel for a long distance. This is the trick Leather always uses. On the bus stop and whenever Oo and Leather are having a break or they are both silent while waiting for the bus. Leather asks all questions about Leather or Ching's business clients' detailed information. After that night's conversation Leather has a thorough understanding of the situation of the region Leather is doing business. It is time to play cunny tricks now!

A few months after the basketball night Leather intentionally stirs up Chit's annoyance towards Leather. It means a quarrel. At that time all working staffs and partners are silent without uttering any single word on every business day. After a few weeks Leather arouses Tense's attention to sit in the office room to watch what is going on. Leather only implies Tense to do it. Never ever tells Tense that there is a quarrel or dispute between Leather and Chit. Tense does his work and reports to Leather that Chit eyed at Tense and other ugly things Chit did while Tense was in the office room. Why Leather asks Tense to do this? Simply at that time Tense is a famous person that everyone believes in what Tense said. Also Leather first leaked the information to Chit and Lez quietly that Tense is going to be a great man in his future life which is expected by Leather at that time. This is not known to Tense yet. This is why Leather uses Tense to work for Leather. After what Tense has spoken something then everyone believes in it. This is to conceal Leather's tricks that Leather intentionally stirs up the dispute.

Fortunately, after a few months the dispute is over. But all is not over yet. Chit and Leather become good partners again. At this time of the year and from then on Chit's impression on Leather is that Leather is a good man, good husband, good father and Chit's good partner. Then the trick come to surface. Leather talks to Ching to close the business. Finally, the business is over. Leather and Chit both got some clients from the partnership company to continue their own business.

Ching is an experienced businessman and occupies lots of businesses. Ching figures Leather stirred up a dispute then closed the company. It is to steal Ching's business clients to become Leather's business clients. By this Leather has many rich clients to buy as many goods as possible. Then Leather is a famous man with huge wealth to show off.

Leather's company is to partner with Lez who knows nothing about business. Lez is a figure head whom Leather can push him to wherever Leather wants. Then after 6 month of business Leather implies Tense to join the company not as a boss but as an office boy. It is to use Tense to challenge Leather's uncle Less not to do harm to Leather at least in a minimum possible ways. During the partnership period with Ching that Less tells Leather to go to his office at night time to sit and chat.

As it is deduced at the first stage Leather tries to work out the intentions of Less on the purpose of asking Leather to sit and chat. Then Leather mentioned those past events to Less which are all on Less's fault. It is Less's idea to do those crimes and evil things. Then Less impliedly promise Leather to become a good uncle and gives some of the family fortunes to Leather. From then on Leather presumes Less repents and listen to Less wherever and whenever what is told by Less to do. Leather cheats the younger son Lance and let Lance to say in public impliedly or overtly that Less repents about his past wrong doings.

It is until the time that Leather's relative Lang comes to talk to Leather on the court case to sue Less. Then Leather resumes to curse Less in front of any person in order to crush Less also because Lang is much more wealthier than Less. These people include Lance, Leather's brother-in-law billionaire Tom and especially Tense. But to Tense Leather is only impliedly saying. Such as whenever Less has done something wrong Leather talks about it in the office where Tense is able to hear what he said. Simply Tense can figure Leather is lying to Leather's own benefits by recalling these events of Less eats up the family business then asks Leather to sit and talk with Less while Leather impliedly announced Less becomes good and now Leather is cursing Less again. This is the trick that Leather always defames Tense who is crazy and analyse any matter in an illogical way.

Why Leather chooses Lez as a partner. Simply Lez has not a single idea on business. Lez only knows the work to do accounting legers. If to hire a bookkeeper to do it. He is certain to be better than Lez. The reason is Lez always stay quiet. Then after 6 months of business Leather impliedly to introduce Tense to the company LL. At that time Tense is studying Economics in a not so famous University. If Tense drops out Tense is not able to obtain the degree but stays in the company LL for the rest of his life. Or after Leather's migration Terri and Tense are left behind. Tense is not able to support Terri. Then they are in deep trouble. Or say it clear Leather wants to crush Terri and Tense once and for all not let them migrate to other places but die in starvation.

Another reason is Lance is studying Business. After graduation Leather relies on Lance to do business for him. If, fortunately Tense is already an economist then involved in any business transaction. Who should Leather listen to? Listen to Lance then Tense will finally notice Leather is not a good father who protects Tense. If listen to Tense it is impossible. Simply Leather always curse Tense as a crazy boy and gives many benefits and privileges to Lance. By that time Lance will be angry and quarrel with Leather. That means a worse situation is waiting there for Leather no matter Leather goes to which side.

To introduce Tense into LL also provides many chances for Leather to show to people publicly that Terri and Tense are crazy. This is a very good excuse to cheat both of them that they are not allowed to migrate to other places. Also to show that they are both useless and a sick patient to let people believe in the pretext they are not welcome to other places. Simply they both cause a lot of problems.

Then after migration Leather under the pretext that he is lonely. Then finds a new wife somewhere else to marry. Then they are both happy and rich for ever and ever, amen.

Again regarding Leather. When Laws is in hospital for the last time. Leather realises from the doctor that Laws is recovering and ready to be discharged from hospital to go home. Leather is very upset and on a Sunday afternoon Leather brings the family for lunch in a restaurant. Upon that lunch is boring. It lasts for 2 hours and no one is talking. Lance even tells Tense, "Tense, it is very boring!". After lunch when they arrive home. As soon as Tense is opening the gate the telephone rings. Leather answers the call and immediately goes out with Terri to the hospital. Laws is dead.

At that time Tense realises this bad news. Tense kneels in the elevating lift to beg God to overturn this misfortune. Everything is done! Dead cannot resurrect. You are not Jesus! From then on as stated Leather has a difficult life. Leather has got 110 shares in the family business while Letton has got 40 shares. After 20 years or so all brothers and sisters sell their shares to their cousin Kim. At that time Leather has only 50 shares. Why?

During these 20 years leather has sold 60 shares to his brother Lns because of financial difficulties. What financial difficulties? All because of Leather's big spending. Leather has a family of four members. Meanwhile Letton also has four altogether. Leather and Letton are both working as employee. Letton is able to go on holidays every year with his family but Leather has to sell his shares to his brother. What's going on, man?

Now Tense,

In the second half of class 7 Tense suddenly has a friend instead of Jik's defamation. This boy Holt is a mean. He says everything to show his friendship but indeed he is using Tense to make him well known in the class. Then attracts many girls and importantly helps him to improve his academic results. Tense is foolish and trusts this boy. At the beginning Tense says anything about himself and a little bit about Tense family. But only to mention Leather is to threaten to reduce Tense pocket money.

As the friendship grows Tense stays with Holt after school. One afternoon Tense stomach is not well and vomits and asks Holt to buy dry lemon sneak for him explaining that after taking in the lemons Tense will be alright. Holt does it but before the lemons come Tense already stopped his vomit. At this stage both of them seems good. Tense as usual a foolish boy follows other people's behaviours since those people are in good relation with Tense. When class 7 finishes then followed by the class 8.

By this time Holt always invite Tense to go to his home with Holt after school. Because Holt has moved. Tense after the summer holidays or after 8 weeks tiresome in the holidays his brain is overworked. It is why Tense feels tired during the day as early as 12 noon. Thus, Tense refuses to go. On one occasion Tense surprisingly says "OK". On the same Saturday afternoon Tense and Holt catch a bus to go to Holt's home.

When Holt gets off the bus he tells Tense this is the terminal. Tense asks him can Tense stay in the bus while waiting in the bus for a return trip. Holt cheats Tense to say "Yes". Suddenly Tense realises it is no good and runs to the bus station to get on the first bus to go home.

Why Tense is overload? Tense joins summer school which starts at 9am then after lunch goes to "Karate class". When Tense is home he watches TV up to 12-midnight. Tense wakes up at 6am the next morning to have marching exercises sometimes at the top of a hill. Usually at a place where it is cool.

All because of the sergeant of St. John Ambulance named Lea wants to show off. He is appointed as sergeant also the top commander cadet. His family is a poor family but his character is always to show off. To attract more girls. Meanwhile he is not loyal to only one girl and feels proud as he thinks all girls love him. No matter this girl is presumed to be his wife or not Lea does all matters he is able to in order to show off and is a rich boy in front of all other people. Especially he always pretends to be a wealthy boy in front of other students especially girls.

At that time it is summer the weather is very hot. Lea lives in a place believed to be hot and uncomfortable. Lea wants to show he is the sergeant to other student and the cadets. He tells the cadets to practise marching nearly every morning during the summer holidays. Either at hill tops or on playgrounds in the college.

Tense has to wake up at 5 or 6am to march then go to summer classes then either to "Karate Class" or "Boy Scout" or see his Medical Doctor in the afternoon and finally watch TV up to 12- midnight. It leads to his stomach to go worse and importantly creates chaos to his neuro-illness which is still not known to Tense and Leather yet.

After that Saturday afternoon Holt does not talk to Tense for a whole term. At first Tense does not understand why. Only before the coming up of examinations Holt secretly phones to Tense and asks some questions such as Karate performance of which Tense is trying to learn at that time. That is on Saturday or Sunday afternoon. On the coming Monday when both of them are back to school Holt still keeps silence but may be secretly talks to other students on something surrounding Tense.

This cause another classmate Ball to ask Tense on one morning before morning assembly. Ball asks, "Did Holt call you first?" Tense nods his head.

Why Ball asks this. All because in that period Ball and Holt are chasing the same girl, Rose in their class. Holt tells other students that Ball said if Ball married Rose. Ball will be having both the girl and Rose's money. At that time Rose is a wealthy girl whose father is rich. Holt wants to destroy Ball's image to Rose.

After the question is asked Ball quarrels with Holt for several mornings before Rose by saying Holt called Tense first not Tense called Holt first. This is to arouse Rose to realise Holt always lies and what Holt said about Ball is not true. So many means! Especially this clan! This college is really a college of means and dirts!

After this incident Tense still does not talk to Holt. When Tense is in hospital because the principal Kwok tells the students in classes 11 and 12L and 12U that Tense will become a great man. That's why Holt plans to meet Tense when Tense is allowed to go back home in the afternoon after consultations during the day. Holt walks with another student along the road where the bus stop is and talking loudly to that student. Tense is stupid to look back only sees Holt is eyeing at him. After all these both Tense and Holt never say a word to the other party. Holt also finishes class 11 and leaves the college with a bad academic results.

Before Holt leaves. He stirs up a quarrel with the physical education teacher to blame the teacher not give Holt a certificate to certify Holt is a student there. This certificate is for Holt to apply other universities. Actually this is true or not only Holt knows. May be it is a pretext to show students he is rich and apply to famous universities.

After these years Tense enters another turning point in his life. Tense is promoted to class 10 but suffers serious illness. Before Christmas that year Leather brings Tense to Dr Ding's residence three times to be diagnosed. All three nights Leather pays the dinner invoice. After Christmas Tense is admitted to hospital.

The first two months in hospital Tense is very scare to take photographs in case someone identifies him in his future carrier. Tense has photographs during picnic times and only before he is discharged Tense finds out he is already in the photos.

During his stay in hospital a male nurse Master You is very good to Tense. You offers Tense to become a captain in football team to compete with another football team. Actually Tense does not want to be captain. No options and Tense does not know he can object. This happens similarly in class 6 when there is a quiz between class A and class B. Tense is appointed as a member in the team. At that time Tense tells himself he knows nothing about current affairs and science materials. He is not suitable nor capable to represent the class to win. The class mistress appoints Tense and Tense does not know why at the time in answering the question that Tense knows the correct answer but says the wrong answer to the umpire.

Tense recovers in 4 months. Leather asks Dr Ding to keep Tense in hospital for another 2 months. Tense does not know why. It should be deduced to be all for Leather's advantages for Leather to process his dirty conspiracy by using Tense. Totally Tense stays in hospital for 6 months.

In the 6 months there is a female patient. She is a movie photographer. When she reaches the level that it is quite alright on her illness. She stirs up a sex scandal among the doctors. Afterwards she is discovered as the mastermind and then discharged some time later.

Before final discharge from hospital there is the Easter public holidays. Dr Ding is planning to go overseas with his family on the holidays. Later it is cancelled may be something wrong. Leather proposes to ask his sisters to visit the doctor. The doctor says "OK".

On that day his sister Leave says she is coming after taking the brother Lawn's family back home from airport. Leave arrives the residence at 4 or 5pm on that day.

When Tense and Leather is in the doctor's residence. Dr Ding sits on a sofa watching TV with frustration. Leather says he is going somewhere and Dr Ding suggests to drive him there. While back home Leave is still not there yet.

In the court room,
"Ms Leave. Did you go to the airport that day?"
"Of course I did."
"Why were you so late?"
"The flight is delayed."
"How long?"
"I waited until late afternoon."
"Then you go to the residence?"
"Yes."

"Since your brother Lawn is right here ready to be cross-examined any time as soon as the court summons him. Are you able to prove what you have said are valid?"

"………………"

"After that day you find out Dr Ding is a friend of the family from Leather. Then you ask Tense to confirm and turn your face black. Is it true?"

"I only want to find out the truth."

"The truth is you want to annoy the doctor not to heal Tense to let Tense to become crazily mad to fulfil your revenge. Is it correct?"

"I cannot recall."

"On that same day there is another lady presents. She is the witness to this question I just asked."

"…………………"

It is because Leave wants to revenge on Leather's cruelty and Tense disobedience to Leave at Tense's childhood. Also Leave has to work out 1 or 2 persons as her targets to express her annoyances since she has not much fortunes from her father Laws. Thus, Leave is doing all she can to destroy these two persons.

CHAPTER 9

After the discharge from hospital and the start of school term. It is in this year that Tense quarrels with Kwok on matters not only relating to boy and girl's love but on many cases such as the conduct of becoming a good man and other matters concerning to become a real gentleman not a hypocrite.

Before admitted to hospital. May be 10 months earlier the brother of Tense that is Lance is sick. Both Lance and Leather quietly and secretly go out together and come back home for 4 or 5 weeks. At that time Tense is busy on the homework. One night before going to sleep Tense recalls what's happening. He realises Lance must be very sick. Then Tense prays to God to let Lance not to die.

A few days later Leather speaks on the phone to a person saying Lance has an illness that no doctor can heal Lance. Fortunately, Lance has a classmate whose father is a doctor. Then Leather and Lance consult this doctor. Afterwards, Lance recovers. Otherwise Lance is sure to die. Years later Lance on the advice of aunts and uncles and his wife. Then these two brothers seem strangers that never meet before and not talk to each other and not even 'Hello'.

After discharge from hospital Tense is introduced to an acupuncture practitioner. At first it is quite alright but after 6 to 8 months the disease is getting worse.

Then Tense goes back to study still class 10 for the 2nd time. In the first term Tense tries to work hard. Only 2 or 3 weeks after the onset of school term Tense is sick. The doctor advises to go to hospital and stays there for 2 weeks without recovery. After this Tense goes to the family doctor who was on holidays that returns home. Tense is cured. After these 2 weeks staying in hospital only watching the walls without doing anything. Tense becomes lazy again.

As the disease is not cured but gets worse. Tense does not revise school lessons any more but only watch TV. At the beginning of the term Tense sees a girl to be assumed beautiful. In the middle of 2nd term this girl Ellen who is studying class 12U and her classmates are leaving or graduated. Tense is very upset and decides to chase her and not let Kwok to discover this secret or to find out.

At first it is OK! All moving smoothly. Finally, the secret is out. Tense at that time under the bad condition of illness decides to declare war on Kwok regardless of Tense himself having any special influences which is granted from Kwok. The war starts. The classmates help Tense in this stage but they are mostly expelled from college by saying their academic results are bad after the final year at high school.

In that summer holidays Tense goes to University Summer School to study. Not really! Tense tells himself he is smart then Fairy will protect him. In case this girl is no good Tense will ultimately separate with Ellen. Actually Ellen is a snake.

Ellen does not have good examination results to enter University. She can go in University is by the introduction of her father who is working there but not a Lecturer. Ellen tells every one whoever she can that Tense is chasing her. That's why when Tense is in summer school Tense is always checked by the student teachers. This trick is inherited from Kwok and later Leather uses it in a more crushing power to Tense as to oblige Tense should under Leather's command. Is Leather a good father?

After the holiday Tense starts medication again and is recovering but slowly. It takes him another year to recover. Ellen keeps an eye on Tense. With the help of college teachers Tense is closely watched by Ellen not Kwok. Kwok is in the darkness without noticing Kwok is under surveillance from his teachers.

At this time of the year Tense is again in class 10. This is the 3rd time in class 10. The class mistress Anne and another teacher Lava is chasing Tense. Anne uses all dirty tricks to induce Tense. Once Anne is teaching in class telling a story. This story implies Tense to quarrel with Leather who is his biological father. Serpent!

In this year Tense losses all confidences. Only to hope Leather applies Tense to another planet to study. Leather has already changed his mind. Leather is planning to send Lance to other planet to study. Not you anymore. Stupid!

At the end of school year Tense goes back to take the school report. Before this Tense has borrowed the note books from other students to revise diligently in summer holidays then pass the examination and go to another worse but still a good college to study and then goes to university. Fortunately, Tense has no report. The report is taken by Leather from Kwok.

Kwok tells Leather to send Tense to another secondary school to study --- again class 10. After this year if Tense gets a good mark then he is welcome to come back to his college to study class 11. Why should Tense return? Simply because at the end of class 11 all students are having a photograph with the principal. That means every one notices Kwok's presence and he is in history for ever and ever amen! Really amen. Because God punishes him and let Tense to flee away from this corrupt college.

At later times Kwok tries all dirty methods to encourage Tense to return to his mother country. Tense refuses. Simply the people are no good. They have a different political system. The most important reason is the people do not like Tense's presence. Only look at Tense's infancy everyone is against Tense. There are so many chaos that make Tense loses confidences. At later life even Tense's uncles and aunts try to persuade or intentionally induce Tense to return. These are only for their own benefits. Again Kwok is sure to have the biggest benefits. It is sure his name will on history by merits of encouraging and to persuade Tense to go back. He is the hero in history. In spite of Tense's misfortunate death or assassination! Only for his own benefits! God, he is your follower, Almighty God!

Before this dispute Tense has power and influences. Tense also notice all students in classes 11, 12L and 12U know his case. No one curse Tense. At least not face to face. But these people are those who keep an eye on Tense not to chase any girl any more. It is Tense to ask classmates of Ellen about her name that these 3 pupils betray Tense to report to Kwok. Kwok creates an atmosphere to Tense to have all power and influence in the college but actually is a slave or prisoner. This trick is later adopted by Ellen and Leather that makes Tense suffers lots of mischiefs, hardships and burdens. This shadow never leaves Tense mind for good.

To the end of school year Kwok tries 3 times to let Tense knows he is in favour of Tense. Kwok stands on the corridor not far away from Tense to look down there to the playground watching students playing same as Tense. This happens two times but Tense does not know. It is the other students tell him afterwards.

On the 3rd occasion Kwok intentionally tells the teacher to stand close to Tense near the end of lesson and to say something to arouse the attention of Tense. Meanwhile Kwok is standing at the door of classroom watching Tense to write notes and study. At that instant Tense really wants to look up. Finally, because of too many notes to write down then Tense does not look up. Again the student sitting next to Tense tells him the story.

Because of these 3 incidents Kwok is very scare and asks Leather to take the report from him and talk to Leather. Why? Kwok still under the image that Leather will send Tense back since the college is a famous college at that time. At this time of the year Leather already plans a schedule to be famous and grab as much power and money as he can by using Tense as a bait for his ambitions. Thus, definitely not letting Tense to return. To be sure!

In the following school year Tense study another secondary school. His best friend Gogo advises Tense no need to work hard. As he understands Tense is working too hard that injures his body. This year is OK. The principal is having the same characters as Kwok to have his name on the history book. They make Tense to repeat. It is only according to Leather's plan that Tense is transferring to another school where Leather can do anything to show his kindness, generosity, the hardships he himself suffered and the love to Tense. These are all void, not valid!

In that summer holidays Leather and Tense travel to another place because his sister Leave is having a baby. In this period Leather intentionally lies to Tense that Tense cannot go to high school in the country simply because the legislation does not allow tourists to transfer to student status. Then finally Tense has to go home. This is an onset of his misfortunes and sufferings which lasts for more than 30 years.

In the summer holidays that Tense goes to summer school in university. Leather and Lance follow the instructions from Kwok to check on Tense. Starting from this period Leather is changing his attitudes to Lance. From then on Leather always brings Lance to dinner with him together whenever someone invites Leather. They do not let Tense know. Leather does not tell Lance to do that face to face. Only in implied body language.

Once they are invited but Tense knows the dinner party. Tense says he wants to go too. Leather immediately express his face showing difficulty in letting Tense to go. In the party Leather asks the host regarding to bring one more person is OK or not. The host happily saying,

"That's good. This party is for children. Many children come is a good idea." Leather says nothing. This shows to Lance that Leather is not willing nor happy to bring Tense but not Lance. Also to indicate Tense that he is not welcome by Leather and not to go out any more. At least not with Leather! God! This is a really good father!

When Tense enters another school "Lee's College". Tense is very happy even without going to study on another planet. Tense works hard every afternoon after school. It is because Tense has a weak body. After 2 months of hardworking Tense collapses. In the afternoon after lunch Tense feels very tired and cannot concentrate on his revision. Later Tense turns on the radio and listen the program every day.

At the beginning Tense supposes to play balls on every Monday afternoon but later calls off. Even feeling fatigue Tense still revises his homework. Two or three months later that is winter time Tense catches a cold and is absent from school for one day.

The next day Tense attends school his classmates all welcome him and talk with him. Tense thinks that now he is having friends. Actually these are teenagers sent by Ellen to disrupt Tense's study to return to St Joseph college. At this time Ellen is the queen of the world. All she says people have to do it. All listen to her.

Ellen tells her followers she wants Tense good and returns to St Joseph. Simply Ellen is graduated in the college she wants Tense does the same. If Tense does what is planned by Ellen, then Ellen has face and that Tense returns and graduated in the same college as hers. Again and again Ellen tells people Tense loves her. Thus, every time Tense talks to girls in class or on the phone that these people know or see. They are not happy.

The day return to school Tense has 2 classmates always talking to him. After their first visit to Tense home. One of the boys says loudly the next day in front of the class that Tense tells him Tense's father is such and such. (A famous and rich person at that time in that place). This is certain to destroy Tense's reputation in class especially to the girls' impressions. Then the girls are not happy to talk to Tense. Finally, Tense has to go back to Ellen.

In the Lee's Tense is studying hard. Before their visit to Leather's sister to see her baby the brother of Terri that is Tom goes to visit Leather. Tom shows off as he is already a rich man or a billionaire. Leather says nothing but is trying to find a chance to become friends again with Tom. Simply Leather is a poor man and have no money and influences at that period of time. Later Leather is called to his paternal uncle Cha to establish a new partnership company to do business which later comes true.

At this stage Leather is becoming rich and goes out with Tom whenever Tom comes to his home. Later both Leather and Lance plan a trick that Lance is chasing Tom's only daughter but a fatal failure.

As Tense is struggling in his study Tom used to appear at Leather's residence and go to dinner altogether. Tense refuses to go together and got money from Leather to have his own dinner. Why Tom suddenly changes his mind? It is because there is a rumour the planet is going to have population explosion some time later. Tom has no place to go. Leather has siblings on other places of the planet. Therefore, Tom wants to go there but needs an excuse. Tom shows off first then with the help of Leather who tells his brother to help Tom while their family is over there after approval of migration.

At the end of class 11 Tense gets 4 subjects passed which is 1 subject in short in order to go to Dun Dun University to study Business. Leather intentionally calls Tense one afternoon to hurry to his friend in that University to see any chance to study Business. Tense is very happy and catch a cab to go there. While Tense is going to wait for a cab Leather suddenly appears to be back home and shows his face to Tense but not utter a single word.

Tense does not get the offer to study. Then Leather plans to insult Tense and calls to University, "You are having Million Dance, aren't you?" in front of Tense one Saturday morning. This is Leather's usual trick to insult Tense all the time.

Later on Leather always telling Tense is a patient who can do nothing and maybe implying to say Tense is waiting to die without doing anything in this world. This happens all the time especially when Leather is angry maybe from his business or private relationships or the rich people show their faces to Leather. Then Leather turns his anger to Tense. Later on used to say it is to test Tense is good or bad and not turning to become bad. Maybe trying to force Tense to do something. Such as to lobby the government to build more universities in the region. Then becomes a famous and Leather has face. Who knows?

Another insult is as follows:

In that summer holidays there is a young man in another retailer shop named Woo who has bought a 2nd hand car and drives to the beach to swim on weekday mornings. Leather joins him together with Lance and Tense and Leather's employee Chung. Tense as usual sleeps late and after answering the phone calls early in the morning goes back to sleep. That's why the team is always late at the beach which the young man is not happy. The young man and his friend ask Tense 2 times the reason why? Both times Tense does not know what to answer and at this moment Leather or Lance is walking to the car ready to go.

When return to Lee's one morning Tense wakes up early and then goes back to sleep. Tense hears that Leather answers the phone by saying, "It is raining and the swim is cancelled. OK. Fine. See you tomorrow."

It means it is Tense to be blamed. It is Tense who did the wrong thing. It is Tense who is a lazy boy. All the wrongs are on Tense which is not on Leather nor Lance. Tense is pure, maybe. Tense does not know why and goes back to sleep.

A Philosopher comments,

Under these circumstances a classmate of Tense once told his friend sitting next to him that the face of Tense is looking very pure. Is it true? Nobody knows. But it is because of this appraisal Tense always thinks he is pure. Such that Tense has many friends and not aware they are means. Such that it takes up Tense's hardships for more than 30 years and never ceases.

During the first year in Lees it is so far so good. Tense works hard in study and in the external examination he scores 4 subjects to pass. In the summer holidays those 2 friends Dan and Ni on the excuse to borrow books from Tense and saying when to return or call Tense again some time later but do not do it. Then afterwards call Tense saying to return the books but all lies. Why they are doing all these? It is Ellen who intentionally tells these followers that Tense will become annoy at the end of the period of the school year. Why annoyed? It is Tense understands those students or any friends are no good or understands they are sent by Ellen. Thus, Tense is not happy and turns his face black. Why on the first instance these friends cheat Tense?

By explaining these Ellen can command people to do this to do that. Also to let the followers to scare and all listen to Ellen as Ellen is looked like a Messiah! Ellen is still in power and everyone hates Tense as Tense is understood to be a bad-hearted person to ruin all good people. Then everyone hates Tense which is what Ellen expects and happy to see as to express her anger to Tense. Why? It is because Ellen has to pretend as a pure girl in front of all other people. By doing this Ellen needs to tell lies and to do anything to let people know she is good. It is hard stuff, man!

On a afternoon Tense receives the same phone call but refuses to take back the books because they are playing Tense. Also at this time Tense is annoy because Fairy does it! To let Tense to know they are bad people to harm Tense. It is Dan called Tense. Then Ni calls Tense telling him Ni is at the corner round there on the street and ask

Tense to go down the street to take back the books. Tense refuses again. Then 3 of them never talk to each other from then on.

At the resumption of school year Dan used to say in front of the whole class he cannot afford to pay the examination fee. Therefore, he is not going to sit the examination. But never talks to Tense face to face any more. Together Dan avoids to see Tense in the corridor or after school. Dan wants Tense to call him first. Nothing happens. In saying Dan has no money. All class-mates realise Tense does not talk and play with Dan again. They will all presume Tense loves money and deserts Dan as Dan is poor. It is to hurt Tense's reputation as no girls love Tense because Tense is means!

CHAPTER 10

A philosopher comments,

The principal Kwok is a bastard actually. He is a snake and teaches other people to do the same nasty things. He used to tell people, "The end is good is good". Oh! My God! Are you teaching us to harm other people or living creatures even to their deaths by any nasty or Nazi methods you are able to implement. God tells us to love your enemy. Some other religion tells them to be brothers and sisters as a whole family. How about you? What are you teaching?

Kwok believes in God. Kwok does anything are opposed to God's teaching. Can we still trust him? God is certain to come to you!

Kwok sends Tense away and welcome back is a trap. The schedule is to let Tense have some burdens which are caused by Kwok. Then returns with good academic results. By that time Kwok is preparing to name Tense as the Head Prefect, gives Tense power and influences. Tense becomes the dominant figure in the college.

In doing this Kwok can show Tense the principle, "The end is good is good". Kwok shows this to Tense that by looking at he himself as a reference. It is a really good example to use the principle "The end is good is good". Again in doing this when Tense becomes a leader in society. Tense implements this principle to all policies and projects. When the historians research to find out why? Then comes to the conclusion it is taught by Kwok. Therefore, Kwok's name is in the history book for good. Clever trick. Nasty bastard! Inhuman animal! Nazi principal!

Every student in that college can be a witness to point out Kwok's cruelties and suppressions from him. No one is going to praise him. To those that praise him is because these students have got some privileges and benefits from Kwok. Even Tense has influence Tense still points out this is a bastard.

In the second year in Lee's it is a clumsy year. At that time Tense is having troubles in his health and private life. Tense writes letters to a radio girl Yee. Tense also stays up late to listen to her program.

The staffs in the radio station are mostly means. They set a trap to make Tense supposed himself has done something wrong but actually it is not. Then use this excuse to blame Tense changes his mind to chase another girl. This causes big problems. It makes Tense never goes out with friends to have a cup of coffee or know other girls except attend school. Also causes Tense not dare to do this or that in case there is misunderstanding.

This affair makes Tense is teased by all people that Tense is coward and incapable. It lasts 2 to 3 years. At last Tense has second thought that Tense has never met this girl. Why should Tense chase her not knowing her characters and her face? This affair is over!

From the departure of Tense in the region that 10 years later. The boss of this radio station re-shuttle the running and personnel in the station. The upcoming director Man expelled those useless staffs and to fire them. These staffs later always accuse Man is not a good manager and put all the blames on this man for any disasters happen in the station.

Why all these happenings cause so much chaos? It is all from the snaked heart of Ellen. From the first year Tense enter Lee's. Ellen sends many teens to Lee's to study. In actual fact they are deemed to go there to destroy Tense's connections with other girls. The most important thing is to let Tense returns to Ellen. Then Ellen is the most powerful lady in this world to do all her retaliations to crush her opponents.

In the event of radio girl affair, it is Ellen finds out Tense listens to radio programs. Then Ellen contacts the radio station with the same excuse Tense is chasing her. Simply Ellen's brother is working in a TV station. The radio people conceals the fact they are quarrelling with Ellen. They pretend listen and believe in what Ellen tells them and causes misunderstandings with Tense. The radio accuses Tense by saying Tense is a wicked man, a man not loyal to his wife, a man cheats the radio girl and a man lusts for money and power.

As Tense does not want to cause any problems. Tense believes in these defamation and gives in. Thus, Tense does not go out and never wear clothes or does anything that is the same as those bad people. Therefore, Ellen sends her men in putting on good clothes and go to restaurants. These Tense is going to evade.

A psychologist predicts by her experience,

Under these circumstances Kwok is used to make himself well known in his society at that time in that place. All Kwok does is to preserve his name in history book. No matter what he always says that he devoted his life time to education even without marriage. These are all lies. If once got married, he has to support his family and children. Therefore, no time or not enough time in education practice. It really means he will not be well known even to his college students.

One more evidence is Kwok used to do anything in front of other people that what he does is upon righteousness without bias. Look at the facts those students from poor family background are certain to be expelled from the college. Look at Tense who is always late for school still survive. In class 8 Tense is late for school every school day.

If Kwok explains Tense is expected to be educated to express his talents in his future life. His late for school can be neglected or deleted. Then why are those students that break school rules face a decision without bias which is sure to be penalised.

Look at this Kwok is strongly objects students to have love affairs. They are certain to be expelled. In a year there is a boy and a girl sit at the very back row every morning assembly. Later Kwok notices this. The girl is gone the next year only the boy remains. In the next year the boy still sits at the back row intentionally to show his anger to Tense of Kwok's cruelty. May be he wants Tense to quarrel with Kwok to let Kwok in a position that whoever cannot save Kwok and surely dead.

Look at another couple a boy and a girl. They both walk in college corridor hand in hand all the time without expulsion from college. Why? Do you know why? The girl is from a rich family. Her family owns 3 or 4 cars with drivers.

Look at the boy. The boy's father is a famous martial arts story writer. His story is so exciting that anybody interested in this type of stories are unconsciously willing to buy at any price.

The boy and girl come from a wealthy and influential background. It is sure they will not be executed and walk out from bars as a free couple.

Upon these incidents what can we say about Kwok's way of teaching in the college? He is good? He is good principal? He is unbiased on anything he does? He is really Judge Kwok? Is he?

On behalf of Tense who is always chasing girls to be sure. But why he has chased so many girls? It is because at that time of the year Tense is always thinking of what methods to know a girl and then to marry. It is because Tense has lost the love from his grandfather and urgently is seeking for some forms of love to fill this vacancy. It is why when Tense is attending classes or Leather introduces girls to Tense. Tense is always to love that girl at that time.

Why is Tense suddenly not pursuing girls at the later period in his life? It is because Tense has decided not to know any girls any more. Decided not to chase any girls.

This is the reason Tense is not keen on girls any more. By the way there are no good girls!

On the part of the snake Ellen who only know playing politics. Ellen tells every pupil in University Tense is in love with her. The facts really show this. After the summer holidays Tense stops to chase Ellen. It leads Ellen has no place to hide. Such as these occurrences Ellen need not to be in love with Tense any more instead concentrate on her study. Then it is OK. Sure?

It is not so straight forward. Simply Ellen is a stupid girl. Her results are not good. She goes into University is by relationship of her father. Her father is a staff in the campus. Most probably Ellen did not score a good result in external examination. Such that she needs her father's help.

After the summer holidays Tense takes in medication again without going to acupuncture practitioner's clinic and slowly recovering. The first year after this incident is a happy year. Without any outside hindrance nor defamation. Close to academic year final examination on one week-night Tense is very happy and goes to market to buy something. When he walks out of the store there is a bus passing through. Inside there is a girl. Later Tense figures out the girl is Ellen. Ellen catches a bus to University.

Why does Ellen do this? She shows to other people she is longing for Tense's love and that's why her academic results are so poor. It shows that she is clever in study but still longing for Tense's love.

At that time Ellen is presumed to be falling from power. But she is a snake to lusts for money, power and influences to dominate this world. This adoption is later picked up by Leather. Ellen needs to stay in power but the university years all other female students were opposing her and regarding her as evil. She has no friends except boy students who are still believing in her lies. Ellen is now in deep trouble!

Again her assignments are no good. She needs to find a way out. Also Ellen always pretends to be pure in front of all people. Ellen passes her 3-year University study and leave the university but may be without a job. Perhaps it is because of her bad academic results. Or on the pretext that she is rich and need not to go to work in any offices. In the coming years she is more harmful than a snake. She shows her purity in front of her men and boys to discuss any possible method to destroy Tense. These cruel methods are all initiated by the followers. Simply Ellen cannot figure out any possible method as she is stupid! At this time, she is not in love. Instead she is full of hatred and a harmful snake towards Tense.

At the time Tense is listening to radio. Ellen lies to the staffs of radio station that Tense is in love with Ellen. Also lies to the teachers in Business class in Summer Holidays on the same pretext. But one day after lessons Tense wants to get a girl's home telephone number. Other girls are asking questions to the Indian teacher. Tense finds a loop and immediately rushes forward to the girl for her telephone number. Fortunately, the Indian Lady notices through the gap between the students.

From this time onwards all people do not trust Ellen. All people know Ellen is a liar. Ellen needs help. Thus, she finds other teenagers through her family members and people working for her to disturb Tense. Ellen pretends to be a pure girl who loves Tense so dearly that Ellen is afraid of Tense's departure from her. This is why Ellen needs people to check on Tense. To keep an eye on Tense with clear indications that Tense has already changed his mind. What Ellen is doing at this period is to harm Tense which is certain! Ellen's methods to lie and tends to be purity are all copied by Leather and his followers at later time in order to cheat Tense. Simply Ellen is very good at lying and to pretend to be good!

This is why this group of people is so deadly criminal offenders at the time. Seems a secret society in the country independent from government control. Later Leather picks up these followers because these people are seeing Ellen has lost power and no one listens to Ellen. Therefore, the followers desert Ellen and turn to Leather.

In the period of Ellen whose followers use every single snake method to destroy Tense. They find any opportunity to insult Tense. Once Tense is on the bus and a boy less than 10 years old intentionally sits next to Tense. At that time the boy's left arm touches Tense right arm. It means Tense is gay without knowing any girls.

Once Tense is working in the company operated by his father and leather's uncle Choy. Whenever Tense is out to the bank or anywhere. These people always shout at Tense's back to say, "Only loves money." In the cases the people suspects Tense might know some girlfriends. Then when Tense is out. They find a chance saying at his back, "It is God's idea."

This means Ellen has got a new boyfriend no need to wait for Tense. But Ellen is still single until she becomes dumb and then dies. The affair with Ellen is going on for 12 years. Unfortunately, God stands behind good people. Tense gets the final victory! Thanks God!

Again one thing as from deduction when Tense knows a girl who is working in TV station. Leather tries all his best to destroy this relationship. The background of the girl Emily is from a democratic country background. Emily learns democracy and fairness in her study. At that time Leather is trying all his best to reinforce his influence in all areas includes TV stations.

This girl is sure to know and tells Tense about Leather's secrets especially his hypocrisy and cruelty towards Tense and his lies and also he sets the traps to let Tense to step inside. Also Leather wants Tense to obey him in straight obedience. All these Emily is going to find out and is most certain to be crushed by Emily. Especially Emily's education is to teach her to become independent. Emily is very certain to prove and persuade Tense to leave the family. At that time Leather will lose everything.

Another case is Leather conspires a secret plan with his brother-in-law Tom to make Tense to chase Tom's daughter Alice. At that time Tense has a girlfriend already. Leather and maybe Tom are waiting to separate Tense and his girlfriend. Then Tense is going to chase Alice who is the only option.

Tense knows this trick as early as they are performing. But Tense figures it is Tom's idea. Tense without knowing the idea is from Leather. Leather is the real master mind. At the end it is a fatal defeat. Tense does not love Alice who is proud and looks down upon people. They never marry and will never marry.

CHAPTER 11

In the court room,

"Mr. Tense, will you please tell me your relationship with your father's family is good or bad?"

"Expectedly very bad."

"Why?"

"They are all hypocrites."

"Are they really?"

"Absolutely!"

"The fact is 'He is your father'?"

"I have no such a father."

"Where do you come from?"

"From my mother's body."

"Why do you so hate your father?"

"It is not hatred. It is fact. He is not deserved to be my father. I am not his son even biologically."

"Really?"

"Of course! My DNA is all coming from my mother. I do not inherit their family's genes."

"I think you ………….."

"I do not inherit the family's characters such as lust for power and money. I do not like to be famous as what is in Leather's mind. All my genes are from my mother. No one else."

"You are one of the favourite grandsons of your grandfather. What do you think?"

"He gives me love. I appreciate. But I already repay the debt."

"What did you do?"

"I listen to him to ignore his own siblings not to talk to them. Also I have helped him in managing the family affairs."

"He is your grandfather."

"Now they both see each other. Are you able to tell me what Leather will reply to his father's questions regarding all matters he did in his life time?"

"I am a Barrister. I am asking you. Mr. Tense."

"I think he has nothing to say. Or simply he cannot reply with real evidence to prove Leather himself is right."

"What are you going to reply to your grandfather?"

"I will tell grandfather exactly what had happened. Again he is not my grandfather any more. I have no connections or relations with this family started from Leather's death."

"What follows?"

"I refuse to belong to that family because there are many reasons."

"What reasons?"

"Their ways of doing things is opposite to mine."

"And what?"

"They do businesses but not report to pay company tax at the end of a financial year."

"And then?"

"They all lust for money, power and reputation. Their children are planned by their parents to marry wealthy sons or rich girls in order to gain influences and many advantages from their wealthy daughter- or son-in-law."

"Your Honour, no further questions."

Quietly and stay alone Tense always tells his mother this story,

Mother I always wish and fancy when Leather was migrating. He was determined to leave you and I behind. If unfortunately, he actually leaves us behind. I prefer to work during the day and study at night or by distance learning.

When I completed the degree I am able to work on my carrier. Then after 3 or 5 years we can apply to other places instead of going with Leather to his destination country. We are free at that time!

Or maybe I know a girl in my work. All three of us can go anywhere anytime as we wish. I have my children and you are a grandmother to be certain!

Regarding my own marriage, I will not marry a wealthy girl. They are arrogant because of her family wealth. I have met one in my study. She comes from a rich family but she is very lazy. Never goes to work in office even there is a job waiting for her which the teacher introduces to this girl. She prefers to stay home doing nothing only hanging around.

The girl is fond of me but I do not love her. I want my wife comes from a poor family where she is used to work hard and struggles to survive. These girls are mostly hoping for a good future which is created by her own hands. Some are exceptions as these lust for luxury and money. They go into university only want to marry to rich family through their university degree certificate as a gateway to accomplish this wealthy desire.

About Gogo whom is Tense's best friend. As soon as Gogo saw Tense at the beginning of their first academic year. Gogo is astonished on Tense's face which shows Tense's purity. In that year Gogo is still a lazy student but their friendship is already building up in a higher and higher level. At that time both Gogo and Tense are living in the same suburb and return home on the same bus after school. Thus, they have plenty of time to talk and chat.

Every time Gogo has got a new pencil or pen or new books or anything his mother has bought to Gogo. Gogo is always giving to Tense to see or read. Then Gogo asks does Tense like this? If 'Yes' Gogo will buy a new pencil for Tense as soon as Gogo arrive home or purchase it after getting off from school bus straight away. Their friendship grows and grows in their 3-year elementary school life. Also at this period it is Tense used to hear Gogo to curse Kwok but Tense does not aware. Actually Gogo's mother was once class-mate with Kwok. Kwok's academic results are not as good as other students. Hence, a Kwok's class-mate who is a lady studied with Kwok while her son is studying in St Joseph with good academic results. This student is expelled from college because of only fails in a simple class test which he got less than a pass mark. His academic results are always on top of the class. Is it revenge or non-biased? God! He believes in God!

Tense understands that Gogo tells him when Gogo was expelled from college which Gogo quarrelled with Kwok in the principal's room. Kwok said he has got lots of school certificates to show his abilities of running a college and capabilities to do all sorts of things. But Gogo argued back that whenever the certificate is dropped on the floor together with a 500-dollar bank note. You supposed which one would be picked up by people instantly?

Gogo knows a lot of Kwok's evil behaviours but keeps very quiet. It is this friendship that lasts for their life time. After migrating overseas they still keep in touch. At first Gogo refuses to. Simply because of his girlfriend. At later date Gogo feels very lonely and depressed. Finally, both of them resumes contact.

CHAPTER 12

Ellen is still sending her teenage boys to disturb Tense. Why she does not send girls? Because once one of the girls sitting at the front row in classroom. Tense looks at her and she looks at Tense. But Tense drops out. Why?

When Tense is learning photography in college. One of the girl classmate Melinda is one or two years older than Tense. Tense gives her a Christmas card. In the meantime, the coach Robert also has tendency towards Melinda. But when notices Tense's desire. Robert withdraws.

Robert is good to Tense or not no one knows. But Robert's withdrawal and he continues to teach the hobby class until maybe after his final year in University. Does he still want to see Tense again? Don't ask me. I totally have no idea. Only Robert knows what he is doing. God knows!

At this time of the year Ellen's hatred to Tense is at top level. Increasing every day and no less. Ellen has to pretend to be a good girl in front of other people. Also she needs to pretend to be smart as Tense. To give an image or impression to others that Ellen is clever and will be a famous woman in the future. At this interval Ellen loses her beauty or attractions and starts to become thinner and thinner. Maybe her family is having financial difficulties. This is the fierce punishments from God, man!

Ellen's brother goes to university and is a big spender. Her brother calls his girlfriend to talk on the phone for 2 hours. It costs a fortune, man! When he comes back after graduation his office work is not good. Many people do the same job and all of them are better than him. He actually has difficulties in supporting his own family after his marriage.

Honestly speaking, is there any good people in this world? From the film 'Omen' the boy screams, "Why is me?" Jesus!

Ellen still does the same thing. After second year in Lee's Tense decided to look for a job. He actually succeeds and the job is working in a blinds and curtain company. He only works for one month as Leather is not happy. Leather tries all methods to force Tense to work in his existing company at that time. The company is partnership with Leather's uncle Choy. Also while Tense is working in this blinds company. Ellen finds an opportunity to contact the boss. Then all senior staffs are on Ellen's side and Tense has no place to stand. It means Tense will be facing a fierce retaliation from Ellen by using the boss's influences.

Why at this time of the year? Leather wants to show Tense is a patient and knows nothing to do nor cannot do anything because he is a patient. Tense is only always loses his temper and nothing else. Also Leather wants to show his paternal love to Tense by demonstrating a perfect father in front of all relatives. This is what he schedules. After 10 years from now Leather is migrating to another place. Then he has the excuse that both his wife and son are patients which their applications are rejected. Leather can go overseas with Lance and then do anything they want.

At present it is to show his love as perfect husband and father. Then in the following year Leather introduces Lance into the company to show Lance's ability and capability to work. After this Lance has pretext to chase Alice.

No matter which son works in the company. Leather never ever teaches them the techniques in doing business. It is later Tense learns it by himself. Why? It is a long ancient story.

When Leather is working in his father Laws's company. Leather is only in charge of the company bank account. Not others. Meanwhile Laws does not treat Leather good. Therefore, Leather wants to gain control of the business. Leather figures a method.

Leather tells his father if Leather continues to only take care of the bank account and control the cash flow in the company. Then Leather knows nothing about business for the rest of his life. Therefore, Leather wants to know techniques to identify what types of jewellery and diamonds is better and affordable by middle-class family. Then to expand the family business. His father says OK. After Leather finished learning from a teacher who is hired by Laws. After that period of time Laws retires and hands down the business to Leather. It is why Leather never teach his sons to learn business.

In the 3 months working in that company Tense does nothing. Only goes out to have some extra food after lunch and going to the bank. As at that time Tense has a fragile body he is not able to work 6 days a week. After 5 weeks Tense always sleeps on the sofa and not able to cook steak as sneak on Saturday nights when got back home. Tense does not know why. He asks Leather but Leather remains silent.

After 3 months Tense decides to quit the job and returns to study. Leather says nothing. His plan is not working smoothly. The following summer holidays Leather pays $600 to Lance from his own pocket to work in the company. While Tense is also working there but no salary.

After another 2 years in the summer holidays Leather goes to see his sister who is having a baby with Tense. Leather lies to Tense that Tense is not able to stay there as a student. Then Tense goes back home and starts studying in Lee's.

In this same holidays Lance works in the company from early in the mornings till nights as told by Leather. The final target is to show to Alice that Lance is hardworking not Tense. Both father and son plan to chase Alice simply Tom is a wealthy man already. Tom invites Leather and Leather's family to picnic in that holidays.

Leather pushes Tense to go somewhere else that is to stay in his sister's home overseas. To let Lance gets a chance. While Alice does not see Tense then Alice is hopefully not to recall Tense is a patient and to reject Lance's proposal.

Tom invites Leather to picnic altogether 3 times. In these 3 occasions Leather intentionally push Tense to somewhere else. Not to be seen by Tom and Alice. This is his conspiracy. Lance has got many chances but all refused by Alice.

After this year in Lee's Tense gets a good result from his examinations. Tense is very happy and continues his schooling. The following year is fatal hazard. He fails in all subjects. Unfortunately, Tense suddenly sees an ad on newspaper one Saturday afternoon. The ad is from a private university from another place. The university Louise College is recruiting new students at that time. Tense is very happy and applies.

In the entrance examination it is to write a composition. Tense only writes 1 or 2 sentences. Tense cannot figure any material to narrate. Tense thinks it is the end of the world. He is finally offered a place to study economics.

Why? It is Ellen. As Ellen went to University is by relationship therefore, Ellen uses this opportunity to let Tense to study university by relationship not by academic results. Then Ellen has all the confidences to tell the world she studies in University does not need to pass any examinations. Only by relationships.

In this year of study Tense works very hard and knows the answers to examination questions. He is the best. Why? The teachers give tips to students. But Tense gets low marks in the report. Why? Honestly, I don't know why! Maybe Ellen lies to the College that Tense does not work hard. Then the College wants him to study therefore, lowers his marks. Maybe? God knows!

At the end of first term Tense knows a girl. The girl grabs the attention of Tense and talks to Tense. A snake. Then Tense pretends to chase her which is ceased only after a few months which Tense works in his father's own company LL Company.

Another student is working in an office but also a student in the College. This man always tells lies to impliedly insult other students and does and says what rich people said and did. This man pretends to be cheerful and helpful but actually is a means.

In the summer holidays this man rings to Tense but Tense has gone to other country. At beginning of the new academic year this man pretends to misunderstand with Tense and not talk to Tense. After a few years Tense meets this man when crossing the road. This man turns his face. Why? He pretends to believe in Ellen's lies on Tense's cruel behaviours that Tense is not a good boyfriend nor a good husband. The man tries to let Tense to beg him for a friendship. This will conceal his hypocrisy. Tense also turns his face to the other side.

Another boy is also not a good boy. This boy always shows off in front of the girls and pretends to befriend with Tense. Later this boy joins the club to harm Tense.

In the second year in the College Leather uses all types of silent language to induce Tense to work in LL. Tense thinks Leather is giving his business to Tense. Tense, on the other hand, is happy to take that. Tense drops out to work in LL. Leather never ever tells Tense he is going to pass his business to Tense face to face. Never! From this moment Tense begins his miserable 4 years in the company. While Ellen losses all her influences and suddenly becomes dumb as myths said.

Leather uses money to induce Tense. First Leather brings Tense to go out for dinner 4 or 5 times. Tense knows something is happening and talks to Leather gladly. Leather only smiles but nothing is said. Leather also asks other family members to say something to induce Tense to work in LL. At first Tense is not willing to work but retains study. Later because Leather's body language and others' dirty sayings. Also Tense is not happy with the students whom are sent by Ellen. Then Tense goes to work in LL.

Leather already plans his timetable. At first Leather stirs up small quarrels with Tense and then pretends to love Tense as a spoiled son also shows to other people about this. Later Leather always insults Tense and the employee Cha with Leather's support shows his face and eyes at Tense.

After moving to new office address Leather starts his plan. On the day moving to new address Leather stirs up a quarrel with Tense. Tense is so annoyed and does not know where to meet Leather to go to new address. Tense goes to new address alone. Suddenly realises Leather might be at old address. Then quickly rush to old address to meet Leather. Before leaving the new premise Tense has a feeling that there are storms and chaos coming. It is true at later date. What method does Tense figures out the turmoils? It is God's idea! It is why Tense is so intelligent simply no one tells Tense what is happening outside. It is Tense to use his mind to figure the exact scenario to deduce what is going on. It seems as those movies that the prophets can foretell the future and the past. It is Fairy and God's mercy to let Tense has this super-natural feeling. Simply all people lie to Tense!

While on the new premises Tense still working happily every day and talks to the employee Cha. At this time of the year Cha is discussing any dirty plans with his brothers and sisters to destroy Tense which is once and for all. The first time Cha sees Tense Cha is already very unhappy and eyes at Tense. Minutes later Cha discovers Tense is the son of the boss then he smiles at Tense.

Why Cha so hates Tense? All because Tense is good looking. Meanwhile Cha finds out Tense is good and kind and every one befriends with Tense. The most important thing is Leather always tells other people in the future Tense will become the leader. This is done secretly and purposefully in order to increase Leather's influences and power in his family and sends a warning to Leather's uncle not to hurt Leather again and again.

Since the case of Kwok in the college. Secondly in the private university. Thirdly in LL. All people are having the impression that Tense is the leader. In these 10 or 15 years Tense becomes very arrogant and will not tolerate any tiny bad words on Tense. But not exactly. Sometimes Tense still tolerate some burdens and difficulties. Such as Kwok's hindrances to chase girls and always repeat in class 10 for 4 times.

It is because the surroundings are in favour to Tense and Tense has mostly positive experiences. Whenever someone says something not good which is indirectly pointing to Tense. Tense becomes angry. Another reason why Tense always quarrel with Leather is both Leather and Tense are in the opposite directions. Tense is good and Leather is bad. There is certain to be chaos.

An example is in the 4 years in LL. Tense always hates Cha whenever Cha shows him his face or anything Cha intentionally wants to annoy Tense then to pretend good to Tense in front of Leather. Why they are always in dispute? It is because Cha is bad! At the onset all people praise Cha is a good boy. Always work hard and kindhearted. In reality Cha is a snake. Why Cha aims at Tense?

Cha is very stupid but he wants to become a boss or manager in any company. It is Tense appearance in LL that disrupts his ambition. Before Tense's presence in LL. Leather likes Cha very much. Tense is told by Terri that Leather used to give Cha 1 or 2 thousand dollars in addition to his wages every time before Leather goes to meet clients overseas.

It is God's framework to show the hypocrisies of those people surrounding Tense to the community. God creates chaos in LL and makes Tense losses his temper then at final stage to demonstrate that is actually a bad man or bad woman. Of course, includes Leather. Why not?

The days in LL is hard stuff for Tense. Every day all people pick on Tense. Those good people all want Tense not to quarrel with Leather. This is Leather's plan! It is until later years the goods find out Leather does not take Tense as beloved son and all things Leather said are false. These people refuse to cooperate with Leather. Leather becomes a lonely man. This is the core reason why Leather closes down his business and hoping to move to another region which needs helps from Lance and Leave who is Leather's sister.

According to the plan Tense is included in the company. Why? At that time Tense has got some supernatural ideas or feelings that Leather needs to destroy Uncle Lang. It is to revenge Lang not to give Leather a larger share of Laws's property after the death of Laws. Secondly, if Tense is working in the company Tense has no time to study. That is no certificates. Then if Tense quarrels with either Leather or Lance and leave the company. Tense cannot find a job. At last, Tense, as supposed by Leather, will come back.

If not, Leather goes to Tense residence to say good words especially shows the face of many worries and sadness and to pacify Tense's angry mood that Lance will not quarrel with Tense any more. This is to induce Tense's return. Will it succeed? Is Tense willing to return after knowing that these hypocrites are already hurting and destroying his self-esteem and self-actualisation. The most important is they are inhuman criminals that all commit offences which they keep secret and only the family members know the truth.

Leather's lethal weapon is to pretend a worry and sad face in front of Tense to show Leather's worry and love to Tense. In reality his beloved son is Lance. Why Leather needs to pretend? All because Leather is fond of Tense from his childhood. It is now Tense is a patient that Leather changes his fond to Lance. But Leather cannot show this to people. Otherwise every one works out his cruelty then Leather is finished.

After some insults to Tense then, Leather turns to cheat Tense by body language that Leather's another brother wants Tense to work as a manager in his company. Then Tense goes overseas. The result is 'NO'. During this stay Tense as usual catches a bus to go everywhere. The second or third outing Tense encounters some fortune tellers. Tense wants to ask for help. On second thought they are good or bad or not? May be they are hypocrites in the same boat as Leather. Thus, the final answer is 'No'.

Then on one afternoon Tense suddenly has an idea to catch other bus routes to other places. This time the bus passes through 2 monasteries. Tense gets off the bus and go to both monasteries to pray. Both prayers are the same. "If 'Fairy can direct me. In future when I am able and capable I will repay the debts to you "Fairy"'. A couple of days later Tense goes back to LL. These are almost all the events written above in the first two years in LL.

Another situation is there is a friend, may be, of Tense, Lady O. She sees Tense's sufferings in LL. Lady O decides to establish a company together with Tense. O has no money but to borrow from LL. When the company is established O can advise Tense that the principal is borrowed money that Tense should concentrate on business, no play. The company nearly sets up. O's father suddenly dies and the plan is called off. In this case the employee is very angry because Tense will be having money and not under Cha's control. Then Cha cannot destroy Tense to fulfil his hatreds. Therefore, one Saturday afternoon when Leather is going out to dinner with clients. While Leather is approaching the door. Cha shouts, 'destroy him'.

From then onwards Cha has more power and even the salary is more than Tense. When the partner in LL tells O that Cha shouts at Tense. O's response is, 'No'. Why the partner does it? The partner is used to be poor. Only this time Leather uses him and makes him as a manager. The incident is timed at the moment that at the time of saying Tense is opening the door to come inside LL office and Leather and Cha are out. This is to show Tense that he is on Tense's side. Always body language! From right here Tense will listen to the partner and the partner can dominate LL. But Tense does not betray Leather and says nothing.

The shoutings from Cha, maybe or most probably authorised by Leather, exactly creates turmoils to Leather. When Terri asks about this incident. Leather simply says Cha is a good employee who earns money for him. Which is more important? Money or son? If you do not sack Cha. It means you love money. Then Tense is no longer your son. Finally, Leather does not fire Cha. This is a good pretext created by Fairy to let Tense leave the family!

On the other hand of this happening and the shoutings of Cha to Tense. All good people work out a solution that Leather is a hypocrite. Especially those riches who are already told by the Chief of the local community. Now Leather has lost almost 90% of what he gained. Leather decides for a migration and close down the business. But as usual, always convinces his partner that Leather will return to do business.

On the days in college and LL Tense is convinced to be a leader. Tense always speaks of politics in front of classmates. Later talks with the people that come up to

LL. Only a little bit. Leather tries several times to induce Tense to go to politics. Tense always misunderstands and thinks that Leather is not happy. After these years Tense decides only to talk or a little bit of discussions on politics. Never ever go to world political stage. Ready to be a simple citizen.

CHAPTER 13

Now it is the turn of Terri. Terri as usual, shouted by Leather to do housework. Before the business company with uncle Choy Terri is full of hatred and revenge. After Tom becomes a billionaire Tom wants migration but does not know any relatives nor friends that can help. Then Tom comes to Leather who has brothers living on another region. First Tom shows his wealth then may be 12 or 15 months later Tom pretends to repent to become a good man. But are these all true? Ask Tom yourself!

Firstly, Leather is still a poor man. Leather wants to befriend with Tom. Therefore, after the dinner where Tense is usually not attending. The next morning Leather says to Tense, 'It does not mean it is smart'. Leather wants Tense to change his mind and go out for dinner whenever Tom invites. Only months later or years later when Leather has money and has the pretext to be brother-in-law with Tom. Leather who is the mastermind sets a trap. At lunch time Tom pretends to slap Stuart's face, Tom's son. Then Leather pretends secretly look at Tense which means Tense is wrong. After this incident Tense tells Leather that Tense will follow Leather's way in all matters and to dine with Tom.

Then on the stage is the film of Lance on the chasing of Alice. Again Lance and Leather both say after Tom has said such and such things. Alice always shows an embarrassed face to reject Lance. On this matter Lance does quarrel with Leather but not dare to let Tense knows the truth.

Before and after Tom's existence Terri is always shouted and ordered to work by Leather. It happens 3 or 4 times already. When Leather's brother and sister return to home place. Leather used to invite them to stay at Leather's home address. Terri as usual told to wash their clothes and socks. Leather's brother Little has shower every night. Every night Little spreads water all over the bathroom which Terri has to clean every day. Little's socks are dirty and dench but Terri still has to wash even with washing machine. Sometimes Little's clothes are told to wash by hand.

No matter what Terri has done. All housework, cleaning, cooking, shopping and buying beverages. All these works are done by Terri alone. The children are young. When they have grown up they go to study. At this time Leather still shouts at Terri. Anything Terri has done or has said are wrong. Leather uses the justifications, impliedly to show, that Terri is not educated to come to conclusion that Terri is talking nonsense. All are illogical and unreasonable. Especially in front of the children Leather adds more dirty affirmations on Terri's doings to accuse Terri.

Terri is treated like a slave or worse than a slave. Why? From the onset Leather does not love Terri. Their marriage is just like a transaction. To buy Laws's trusts on Leather. In return Leather demonstrates his ability to become a good husband and most important a good son that receive father's business.

Look at Lance. Lance chases Alice is simply because Tom is a billionaire. A good transaction. Both Lance and Leather are happy. Once Tense mentions he knows a rich girl but refuses her love. Leather's reply is in a calm mood. Telling she is rich is not a problem. Then curses Tense that he will not get married under these conditions especially as a patient. Good business! Good profits!

Another rich girl wants Tense. Her father contacts Leather that always go out for lunch. The daughter is very proud of her father's fortune and never say sorry or never apologise to any person. Her father tries to link them together. Leather deceives Tense by talking anything in favour of Tense during the lunch. Seems Leather is on Tense side. Actually, Leather is the mastermind!

Under these deceptions Terri is not willing to marry Leather. Leather obliges Terri by telling the restaurant is booked, invitation cards are all sent out to friends and relatives. Then Terri must marry Leather. This is illegal, man! Your genes are all favoured to criminal activities, includes all your family members! What is your opinion? Can you prove it, man?

After the born of both sons Terri still does all housework non-stop. The obstetrician advises to take a rest not doing any work. Leather considers it is a joke. Never follows. Who is Terri, man? Is she your wife? She is a slave under your control? You are indeed not in love with Terri. Your marriage is a business transaction, man! Prove this is wrong! Can you?

God is fair! When Leather is sick and admitted to hospital for surgery. The surgeon does a bad job. Every time there is a minor mistake. Leather needs to undergo surgery for three times in total. God's miracle! Why?

Once Terri has something stick in her left eye. Leather drives her to local doctor who sends Terri to an eye specialist. This is a simple surgery even a General Practitioner can fill the job. But not him! Why? Ask somebody yourself. Don't ask me. I do not know his academic results!

After the specialist completes his job. The specialist says Terri needs to go home straight away not to have problems. Leather drives all of them, Terri and Tense, to Leather's favourite suburb going here and there in the whole afternoon. Then comes to a chemist to buy Leather's pills. The pharmacist asks what happened to her eye. It looks like ulcer. Then Leather goes to one more place and drives home.

Another happening is when Tense has a scar on his inner left thigh. Leather drives to that doctor's clinic. Before this no one says anything. During consultation the doctor suddenly cuts the scar and causes pain on the thigh. The doctor insists there is no iodine in the clinic to put on the surgery. After this Leather drives to buy a new lamp to put on the kitchen ceiling. After he has already parked the car Leather hurries to walk very fast. Tense needs to rush to follow him. The surgery causes him very sore. Later Tense quarrel with Leather by saying Tense's thigh is sore but Leather still walks fast. Leather says he does not realise.

Is Leather a good husband? A good father? A good son?

When Laws is sick Leather hires a doctor to take care of Laws in hospital. After 2 or 3 weeks Laws is recovering and is very happy to look forward to play with Lance.

On Sunday afternoon Leather brings the family out to lunch. This lunch is really lunch! It takes more than 2 hours to complete. When back home the phone call tells Leather that Laws is dead.

After 3 or 4 months Leather used to mention to any person that the doctor took care of Laws is a good doctor. Simply everyone agrees. But those under her consultations all disagree. Leather used to tell anyone that he is brought up in the family office. At the start Leather is still an account keeper but in that episode there are many types of people go to the office to visit or asks for help. Leather tells his sons that Leather has seen those bad sons who steal other siblings' money after their father's death or a family court battle when the family is not in harmony. Leather has seen these many times and Leather will understand a person's attitude is tending to be good or bad only after talking to that person once.

This doctor who Leather does not identify she is no good. On that afternoon Leather and his own family goes to lunch. Why? I do not know why! Ask another person!

Another occasion when Tense is chasing the TV girl. Leather confirms to other people in public that his family members the Lung family members all are working on any issue. No one is a lazy person. Everyone has to do some work. The TV girl shows she is hardworking. Leather insists to separate this couple.

On the contrary, is Leather a hardworking person? From the beginning of his marriage till his death. Leather never does any housework. All are done by Terri. Leather only sit on the sofa reading newspaper. Later years Leather wants to expose his diligence. Leather washes the floor together with Terri. When Tense is home at that instant. Leather pretends his body is not in a proper way that makes him very uncomfortable and painful. Why? He wants Tense to assist in the cleaning that Leather does not need to work any more. Is he a good man? God knows!

In the final days of Leather who still wants to be on the top of the world. He secretly conspires with Lance to shout at Terri. Condemning Terri has bad table manners every night. When Terri is working during the day Lance used to disappear and is not home. On this occasion Lance does not need to help to work and avoid doing something wrong that Tense has pretexts to complain Lance. On the behalf of Leather who is the master mind. Leather never scolds Lance's behaviours. Only says "don't do this to mother" for once and then keeps very quiet.

It creates chaos in Terri as she is already a neurological patient and not educated. It arouses fear in Terri's mind. Later it is OK. Goes back to normal. Why? Because of the aid of Tense. Tense always encourages Terri not to be threatened by Lance. Lance is not correct to shout at mother. Tense encourages Terri not to worry nor frightened. Later time because Lance borrows money to do his business but fails. It let Leather has to borrow money from relatives that makes up hatreds and blames towards Lance from Leather. Leather tries to calm down Terri not to fear. Still dirty trick. Why dirty trick? Leather only wants to revenge which the consolation is not going to help Terri to recover her self-esteem but aims retaliations on Lance.

Terri always goes to monasteries for her religion. Leather only drives Terri to the address and goes to lunch or returns home. Never step into the monasteries. Only at the time Leather wants to recover from fatal illness then he does go there. Leather wants to leave and not to go to monastery any more after his illness is recovered. Therefore, Leather conceals Tense that the monk was saying Leather will not come back after all his illness is right. Leather puts the blame on the monk. This is his usual trick.

Whenever he is wrong he first says someone is doing the wrong thing that Leather is committing. Such as Leather refuses to go to monastery after recovery from illness. This is what is in Leather's mind. But Leather come out to say someone said this. It is to conceal Leather's cruelties. In this case whenever Leather is recovered. Leather needs not to worship in monastery. He is already a healthy man! No need to monastery anymore! Correct? God really knows, man! Is Leather a good follower? He does not go to monasteries, not give money to beggars on New Year Day, humiliates Terri and Tense especially after someone has already humiliated him and retaliates to Terri and Tense, does not support Tense but stands on the side of the employee Cha. All these are inhuman animal nasty characters. Leather even does not do housework at home!

When Leather's brothers and sisters stay at his residence. All clothes are washed by Terri as stated before. Terri works at home non-stop. Leather does not ask or discuss with Terri to do housework. Leather orders Terri to wash, to cook and to clean. Every day stays home to do all the work. Terri works in such huge loads that leads her hands and fingers lose mantle acid which needs moisturising cream to recover. Is he human? Those brothers and sisters stay at his home never ever say "Thank you!" to Terri. Instead they suppose Terri is a dog or calf to work under their command which is correct. Is this correct?

There is a fact that Leather's grandmother and his two sisters tells him to move out of the family home which he rejects. Later Leather tells his brother that Leather won't talk to these 2 sisters again but not Leather's father.

In later years Leather always shows a smiling face to these sisters and their husbands. Why? At that time episode they are richer than Leather. Leather is not able to play any trick. When the whole big family resides in the same area overseas. Leather before going there or before migrating there he tells Terri that Leather is going to restore harmony with these 2 sisters. Why? There is power struggle right there and Leather badly needs supports and trusts from his siblings. Even though Leather knows beforehand that his siblings are also mean people same as him. Does he love Terri? Does he love his son Tense? Leather only loves money and power! Is it correct?

When Tense is in LL. Those conversations between Tense and Leather which is Tense showing and telling Leather that someone is an evil. Leather immediately tells that person what Tense has said to Leather which he/she is evil. Also emphases that Tense is always doing the wrong thing as a neurological patient and does not able to distinguish good and bad and always thinks in an illogical manner. Why Leather does this? Leather is trying to stir up chaos in Tense then pretend to love Tense that goes here and there to ask for help in order to help Tense. By doing this Leather is always praised as 'Good father and good husband'. Not God father, really!

Even Tense is working in LL. Tense is only an employee not the boss. No official title! And always humiliated by employee. Whenever Leather goes to another region and starts business to include Tense as director in the company. It is only to pretend to be good to Tense! Tense's job is to go to the bank to deposit money and answer the phone. No more! All decisions are made up by Leather and Lance. Only you!

From the beginning to the end Leather never discusses anything with Tense but Leather's siblings and son Lance. They plan a wicked trap and conspire a procedure to let Tense steps into it. If Tense is annoyed they put forward the pretext that it is to test Tense is good or not. Once Leather intentionally conceals his ugly face by saying to Tense 'It is for your own good'. Tense's good or Leather's good? Please explain!

Leather very often uses tricks to pretend to be a good man in front of his father, sisters and brothers. Of course, in front of Terri. When Tense is young he is the beloved son of Leather because Tense is the fond of his grandfather. After Tense diagnosed of illness Leather immediately turns his care to Lance. Leather's sisters insult and humiliate Terri. Leather still says he wants to return to harmony with them. What do all these mean? A good husband? A good father? Maybe a mean person! An inhuman monster and family! Is it correct? You make your decision. Right or wrong!

Terri is a good mother who cares for her children. After marriage Leather tells Terri do not bother the children. Leather will take care of them. How do you take care, man? One goes to hospital and the other one goes out to play every day. Is this a good education?

Before the first external examination Leather asks the class mistress what is the chance that Tense will pass the examination. The teacher tells him should be 90%. Leather tells his friends 80% and Tense 70%. What do you mean? You are only able to control people and slave them. You are not educated. Terri is not educated but Terri learned from her mother to care for the children. Did your mother teach you this? Your mother only gave you power which you manipulated in a terrible mood to keep tight control of your brothers and sisters. So horrible that it is colder than ice water. Ice Age!

You always use the excuse that Terri wants revenge is not correct. Terri works days after days and still has to be cursed by your good sisters. Terri is so annoyed that she cries in her bedroom. 10 years later Terri needs to go to hospital. If you were Terri. What are you going to do? Only smile and let it go? Excuse me, man!

You humiliate Terri and Tense whenever you like. You keep a tight control on Tense. Especially on his financial condition. You give Lance $500 every time he asks for it.

If you were they what are your responses? Let it go? You and your sisters' relationship that you will prefer to let it go. Why? It is because they are rich. They are much wealthier than you. This makes you need to smile at them and say "Hello" every time you both meet. Why did you quarrel with your sister in the family meeting about the distribution of your father's Last Will and your father's fortunes? I tell you something, man. It is better to be a good man than to become an evil man.

CHAPTER 14

In the second year when Tense is still in LL. It turns around but still under devil command or in monster centration camp. Before this time every one picks on Tense every day. Tense losses his mood and later return to silent mood. What silent mood? At first Tense used to talk and talk all the time. In LL Leather and other people show their faces, curse Tense and keep Tense in the dark by not let him know anything. Tense does not know anything what should he do in response? Your pretext is to test Tense is a good man or not. Actually you need to certify you are a good man or not, man!

After the 2 incidents in the monasteries where Tense prayed to Fairy for their directions of what to do next. Tense goes back home and forget it. A couple of weeks later Tense very often to have nightmare and shouts out loudly but Tense does not realise. Leather still as usual not to say a word. Instead always scolds and gives hardships to Tense. After a few weeks Leather pretends as a good father, usual trick, to quarrel with Tense then spell out Tense has a turmoil mind and under pressure.

On that night Tense again has nightmare and shouts. This time Tense is awake and remember what Leather has said. To return status of quo Tense walks to the kitchen to drink water. From then on Tense has nightmare or actually has dreams that exactly comes true during the day. Tense says it is supernatural feeling.

From this time onward Tense' friends, are they real friends? They smile and courtesy to Tense. Cha is very angry but not mention a word. Cha still on the framework to destroy Tense. At this time Tense suddenly got an idea to learn martial arts. Tense has already done the exercise of Martial Arts in the morning before goes to work. The exercise is really good. It takes Tense to transform to a strong body. Leather learns about this, as usual, sends other people to persuade Tense to keep on Martial Arts training. Why? All ugly tricks!

Leather wants Tense to work up to Master. Why? Simply because if Tense was a Master meanwhile other fighters are jealous. They will come up to the Martial Arts Academy to stir up quarrels and then leads to a fight. If fortunately, Tense losses the battle. Tense will become handicapped or disabled. Now Leather is able to demonstrate his deep concern to Tense. The most important thing is to pass the business to Lance.

In this Martial Arts training session Leather as usual introduces a girl to Tense. The training only lasts one month and Tense is thrown out. No one tells or explains why but thrown out! Leather again introduce another girl. Tense is so annoyed that he prefers to stay with that girl Pat only on retaliation and does not fall in love with Pat. Only to pretend and only this time! How about the employee Cha? At this time Cha has a holiday. On his return he losses power because Tense uses silence strategy to tell Leather during a lunch meal while Leather is talking about the employee with his business partner Yan. After Cha's return he does not know why suddenly no one tells him anything about Tense. Cha starts to create disturbances after discussions with his brothers and sisters on the previous night and does it on the following day.

Cha dares not disturb Leather but not Tense. In the mornings Cha goes to LL to work. Early morning no one comes back to office yet. Cha uses body language to first blackmail Tense. Later finds out Tense is not afraid. Then he used to smile to Tense while Tense is boiling water or come back from outside or back from toilet. Cha wants to show he is a friend. But why at this time? Cha's father was admitted to hospital of respiratory system defects. Cha needs to find out is his father going to die? If 'Yes' Cha has to do some work to prepare for his brothers' attack as they are not in concord.

How can Cha find out? Tense has dreams at night therefore, Tense is the only option, no other resources! With this incident Cha and his siblings have used up all their savings. They have no money to show off to Tense. They remain quiet. The only alternative! Cha retains silence for another 2 years until Leather migrates to another region. Cha wants to migrate too. But now he is not Leather's favourite then his choice is only to pretend a good boy to work hard. No options. Does he? Hoping one day Leather changes his mind and apply Cha to go there with Leather. Will Leather do this? Leather is much narrow minded than Cha. Cha's pretence makes Leather has no face as Leather appears to be a genius. Cha makes Leather losses face and Cha's pretence is better than Leather. Leather is afraid Cha one day will stab at his back. Does he remember his father's death?

These 4 years are in hell! Tense has no happy days since Ellen's disturbance. In these 4 years as Tense understands it is Leather who contacts any person Leather knows or meets to become his agent. First, Leather tells these people Tense is always happy and always makes jokes with others. This is to let them feel happy and funny.

Secondly, Leather tells them Tense has got supernatural feelings that most of the times they come true. Tense also will beg Fairy to protect good people. All these arouse the followers envy and induce their tendencies to support Leather. One important point is they can be agents to keep an eye on Tense that they are in a higher position than Tense to control Tense but Tense only knows they are good people. Not bad! Really? Stupid man!

What are those people? They used to come from poor families and not educated. The noisiest people are TV stars. They pick on Tense every day and accuse Tense is an arrogant person as having supernatural feelings which Tense's characters and his doings are not. Their method is to put all the blames on Tense and insists it is done by Tense. A scape-goat!

Whenever they have difficulties they go to Leather and Leather turns to Tense. Once Tense knows something is going to happen but do not know what. Leather stirs up a quarrel with Tense. A few days later Leather talks to Tense as a good father. Tense tells Leather there is something but Tense is not going to do it. If Leather wants to do it Tense tells Leather to do it himself. Leather has no face!

Why Tense does not help Leather? From the start Tense already known the matter is illegal! How can Tense help? To help means you are also a criminal offender and sentenced to jail. Thus, from then on Leather changes his tactics. As Tense knows something is in trouble but does not lose his temper. Whenever Leather and his followers have problems they show an angry face to Tense and pretend to ask for help but never beg Tense to help. By doing this Leather has face and never tells Tense that it is not lawful. If Tense is angry of whatsoever reasons they will say it is a test to see Tense is going to the wrong way or not! Really good people! Alternatively, Leather pretends not to know the truth but because of Tense's annoyance which makes Leather realises something is going wrong! Good man! Really good! God!

CHAPTER 15

From now on Tense is the most famous and favourite son of Leather. Leather first wants to crush Tense to his worst situation as possible. When Tense loses his self-esteem and self-actualisation Leather will set a trap to oblige Tense to follow Leather's way of doing things and the axiom is "The end is good is good". Leather and later Lance both together try many times to let Tense feels which Tense is great and a national leader. Why? Simply because if Tense involves in those not necessarily politics involvements but in the current affairs of the community. Tense is famous then Leather is famous too. At that time Tense always misunderstands Leather's opinion is "don't go to politics". Together Tense always tells himself that politics is dirty and un-conscience. At least in some countries it is. Leather tries hard for 2 years but still not able to arouse Tense to touch any politics.

Abruptly Tense has got the supernatural feelings which is to Leather's best possible weapon against his uncle Lang. It is to revenge Lang did not give more cash and property to Leather but to Leather's brother after Laws' death. As at that time Leather's cousin Long is by now conspiring to sue Lang. Lang did hurtful things to Long and his brothers after their father's death. Also Lang did and does many criminal offences with his 2 sons. Such as to steal the company money to set up their own business. They took more than 20 million dollars from the family business at that time. Therefore, this is the right time for retaliation.

In the first 2 years of life in LL. Tense is living in hell. Leather's favourite tack is to disturb you into chaos then ruins you into much more worse circumstances and havoc. Leather wants to see you as worst as possible. Alternatively, if Leather in at an underhand position. Leather will do whatever you tell him. As a slave! But if you tell him to knell down and beg you. Leather pretends to have self-esteem and refuses. Fortunately, if you disclose to him to impair his biological sons. Leather is happy to do that. But done it secretly and quietly not to let anyone notice such that he is still a gentleman in front of other people especially Terri and Tense.

Look at that whenever Leather borrows money from Hung, Leather's brother-in-law. Hung is usual and always goes to have a chat with Terri. Meanwhile Hung's wife never appears on the spot. At that time Terri supposes Hung is kind and good to her. Later Tense explains to Terri that Hung is a man to play ladies. But every time in these occasions Leather is either in his bedroom or somewhere else that no one knows where he is. As it is Leather still visits Hung and always humiliated by Hung and his sons. Leather pretends not know and just talk and talk. In reality, Leather is trying to work out their motives which are good or bad to Leather. Such that Leather is able to revenge to them in a crucial or minor way in future. It is that why Leather still goes there to be disgrace. When Leather is at the premise Leather knows how they hurt Leather and who is the most harmful. When Leather is again capable and able to. It comes Leather's retributions. This is the Lung Family characters, to be crystal clear.

Leather and Kwok both put Tense as the most important person of this world. This they can work out Tense' political ideology and fill in their ambitious desire to suit Tense. Both want to be famous and their name are in history books for ever and ever! Beautiful tricks! God is more intelligent than you both. God will not allow unacceptable plans happen in this world to injure people and these people are defected to a pitiful or condolence situation. Leather has a more ambitious desire is to be the first emperor of his family in this material world. Good luck!

To conclude in the second two-year period in company LL Tense is quite alright without any insults. Everyone is good to Tense and a friend of Tense. What is in their minds? You know! I know! God knows! In this period Tense knows a girl Ether who is a worker in a financial company FF. But again conclusion is in sympathy.

Tense knows Ether is by Tense himself not introduced by Leather. Leather is very angry. Leather wants a retribution. Why? It is because Tense chases this girl with all his heart. Before this Tense's girlfriends are introduced by Leather (through Leather's followers). Whenever there is argument or disagreement Tense is definitely to withdraw and ends up to separate with the girl. This time this girl Ether is known by Tense himself. No matter what quarrels Leather stirs up on the day Tense goes to the financial company Tense will not say anything worse but only with a non-smiling face while talking to Ether. That's why Leather is so angry. At later stage Leather is to set a trap to separate them for ever. Tense at this period is still very foolish thinking Leather is happy with this girl. Therefore, Tense continues to pursue her.

Why Leather let her go? It's because Ether is a lazy girl. On Sundays she is always as usual to invite her working colleagues to her home address to gamble. That is no work! Another reason is Ether is a big spender. She buys bracelets, watches and even necklaces as many as possible. Leather uses this buying useless decorative on females to induce Tense to spend lots of money to purchase the materials Tense likes. By spending so much money Tense will be a poor man. Leather can set down financial constraints to make Tense feels he is poor. Then there will be insults and also Tense cannot go to study nor go out for dinner on his own. That means Tense will not have friends or classmates to talk with and the most important thing is no girlfriends. Thus, Tense will be happy to chase any girls Leather introduce. These girls all are, or must, obey Leather. It means Leather is still the mastermind of anything in this world.

The affair continues or looks like to continue smoothly. After Tense's migration to another country Tense still writes letters to Ether but always no reply. Then on one summer day Tense receives a return letter saying Ether has resigned, left the company or even migration to another country. Is it true? Who knows? Better ask Leather, man! But you still got the void answer. To be sure, man!

While Leather and Tense has not migrated yet. Leather tends to bring Terri and Tense to Tom's home to have dinner. The target is to let Tense have chances to see Alice, Tom's only daughter then chase Alice. Tense as foolish as before does not know. One thing Tense understands is Alice is in love with Tense. That's why when once Alice has a good salute to Tense. Tense replies, "Good girl!" to finish her day dream. Tense still does not know it is Leather who is the mastermind.

Later onwards after migration Tom used to invite Leather to lunch and dinner. During the meal Tom talks and talks. Tense understands Tom's motive is to bring Tense to chase Alice. But what is in Tense's mind? Tense is not able to chase another girl while Tense is having a girl friend or a wife. It is utterly not conscience! A man cannot throw out his legal wife and chase another girl simply that girl has money or power or influence which your wife has not. Tense does not know these are all conspired by Leather. Leather is the master mind, indeed! Thus, Tense has a bad impression on Tom!

CHAPTER 16

After Terri, Tense, Lance and Leather have all migrated to country on another Continent. Tense thinks and hoping a new era and smooth no sufferings is coming. Leather still manipulating his conspiracy. Still wants to be the most powerful man on earth. At this time of year Leather's followers are far and far away on another region of the planet. Leather's brothers and sisters all do not listen to him. This is stated before that Leather will be compromising with his 2 sisters to return to harmony. On Tense's behalf Tense still wants to study then find a job. But Tense cannot. Why?

It is all about Tense's illness. The doctor on this newfoundland is a bastard. The doctor prescribes poisonous medications to his patients. When the patient is feeling something wrong. The doctor says it's OK. Only after 4 or 6 years the doctor Dr De pretends to work out your problem and prescribes a medication for you to recover. From then onwards you trust him very much and he is sure that you will come back for consultations. Again this is what Leather asks Dr De not to prescribe medication. Both men are on the same boat. Whenever Tense is sick. Tense cannot go to find a job. Cannot go to study. That means Tense has no friends therefore, whenever Tense has got a problem. Tense only option is to beg the Lung family. No choice!

Three or four years after staying on this Country. Tense once tells Leather that Tense is going to have good luck. Therefore, Leather immediately introduce a girl to Tense. At first Tense refuses. On second thought Tense realises Tense has to say 'Yes' at last. Then Tense has this affair.

During this affair Tense's sickness is going from bad to worse. At first Leather always supports and encourages Tense on this affair. Tense is in puzzle. Why? May be the girl is a good girl. Later found out the girl used to listen to Leather and does what he said. After a year Leather finds out the girl Moveea does not tell Leather of what Tense has told her. Leather is already preparing a trick to separate them as retaliation.

Six or seven months later when the lie is forgotten by Moveea. Leather suddenly asks Moveea to decide to marry or not. The following week Moveea replies 'No'. Then Leather tells Tense to discontinue the affair. At this time Tense has a feeling that Tense needs to find out why. But Tense does not love Moveea from the very beginning. Why Tense has this feeling? Tense is not able to figure himself. God knows! After Leather's death Tense finally separates with Moveea.

The reason why Tense is not able to control his behaviours but insists to the affair with Moveea may be from his natural feelings. Tense is controlled by this feeling to continue the affair because Leather is going to die. Before his death it is a good idea to concentrate on a girl to deviate Leather's targets not to disturb Tense. Thus, Tense has a better circumstance to act on instead of insults from Leather. Then after Leather's death they are separate for good! God!

Before Leather's death Leather is always out to his brothers and sisters' home to sit down to have a gossip. At this time Leather still recruits followers for future operations. On such a situation it is not the same as before. Those followers break his arms or some become dumb. All of them finally refuse to further help offered to Leather.

Right at this time the former followers also migrate to this country. They come forward to Leather. First is the manager of a restaurant Mr Deng who introduce a girl to Tense and supports Leather. Tense does not like that girl. From start to end both of them never talk to each other. Later Mr Deng quarrels with Leather. May be regarding who is the first to give commands. A power struggle. Leather sets a trap to accuse Deng did not serve what Deng was told. Leather says this matter to the big boss. Deng is fired later on.

When Leather is doing business in his home town before migration. It is because another retailer Mr Wung disagree with what Leather has done. Leather accuses Wung to have an invalid ledger to report to the Taxation Office. Wung is very annoy at the time and walks away. As soon as he realises Tense is standing in vicinity. Wung immediately returns to Leather to explain.

Another retailer Good Office the boss is Kime. Kime once conspires with Leather to induce Tense to chase a girl Lem. First Kime insults Tense and then shows Tense or tries to lead Tense to chase Lem. At that time Tense does not know what is going on. If Tense is going to chase Lem. Kime pretends to chase Lem too. Whenever Tense succeeds and Tense and Lem get married. Kime always tells Lem to persuade Tense to give benefits to whatever Kime is doing. If not Lem will say Tense is doing revenge because Kime was once Tense's rivalry. At this stage whatever Kime is doing or Leather is doing. They all succeed even doing criminal offences!

Later on Wung never ever goes to lunch with Kime simply Kime is not doing things properly.

Another point every girl Leather introduces to Tense is that they all eat chickens. It is the religious rule not to eat chickens on Tense's behalf. Why? Simply Leather uses the girl to show to Tense to break the religious rule. Then shows to Tense he has already broken the religious rule. It does not matter anymore at this time of the year to break the country's legislation and becomes a criminal offender. Cunny wolf! Unfortunately, Tense does not break any legislations either religious or country laws! It is God's power to direct Tense to do the right thing, mate!

At some time of the year the general medical doctor Dr Six and the Vice Principal of Lees Mr Hox does try to persuade Tense to go out to see the world. To greet more friends or go to play a sport or transfers to another High School to bet Tense's own future fate! Also may be Hox realises Leather's hypocrisy that encourage Tense to go out which to cease Leather's intervention on the College affair. But at that time of the year Tense is not dare to go. Also Tense has not got any method to retaliate to Ellen's inhuman attacks. What can Tense do, then? Sit and watch and waiting to be insulted!

By this time many people have come to this country and continue to do what they have done in the past. They still pretend to support Tense but actually they are doing crimes. It is because at this time Leather and his brother has no money. They need to find a person who is rich to support Leather in case there is a court case. They find Tom.

First Leather sets a trap to mislead Tom of thinking himself is already not strong enough to do business. Then Tom as deceived closes down his business. After sometime Letton is renovating his house. Meanwhile Tom is building his new house. Tom visits Leather nearly every night to talk about his project. Letton goes for a walk at night and sees Tom's car is parking outside Leather's house. On one night Letton drops in to talk about Letton's house. Why they both ask Leather? Leather has built 2 buildings when he was young.

This is to demonstrate Leather is not happy with Tom but Leather is also still having a lot of money and lots of support from his brother. This is to tell Tom to join the group. Tom understands. Later they do not see each other again.

Leather used to say Tense is not a good boy. What Tense does? What Leather has done? Who is good? Who is bad? Have you ever heard God will commit crimes? Or Jesus is harming the innocence? They are God. They will not do evil things. It is you Leather, an evil spirit who is sure to commit crimes. It is 100% sure!

In the court room,

"Mr Leather, can you recall on one night at that time is around 12-midnight. There is a phone call from Tense's friend Gogo. At that night it is you who first answer the call. Gogo tells you he is calling from overseas in a country called Strengths. He also mentions Tense's old name "Moore". Is that true?"

"I can't recall."

"After a few years your sister Lie goes to Strengths with her family and Tense's cousins for holidays. Is it true?"

"I have no idea!"

"When Lie is in Strengths does she and the rest of the group go to look for Gogo from the address Gogo writes on the replied letters to Tense?"

"I have no idea!"

"Again after another few years you quarrel with Tense. A few days later Tense tells you he is going to do business with Gogo. Is that right?"

"I can't recall!"

"Tense tells you Tense is going to sell office equipment sent from Gogo to sell in this country. Is it correct?

"At that time your response is to tell Tense that Gogo is cheating Tense's money. Is it correct?"

"……………………"

"At that time you also mentions that it is from the dialogue between Gogo and Tense that you figure out

Gogo is trying to deceive Tense in this business. Is it correct, Mr Leather?"

"I can't recall!"

"In this case how do you find out Gogo is trying to cheat Tense's money?"

"I………..I……….I……….."

"Do you send people to follow Tense wherever Tense is going?"

"No, I do not."

"How can you find out Gogo's tricks?"

"……………I…………..I………….."

"Do you send people follow Tense?"

"………Well…………Ah,……Yes……..Ah………Well………"

"If you send people follow Tense. Do those people tell you about this business dealing?"

"Well!…………. A h……………Yes………Ah…………No………Ah……."

"If "Yes". How do they find it out?"

" W e l l … … … … … . . A h … … … … … . Well…………….."

"Do they tell you this, Mr Leather?"

"Well……………Yes………….Well…………Well…………."

"How do they find it out, Mr Leather?"

"………………Well………………..."

"How do you know Gogo's address in Strengths?"

"Well……………I……………"

"Do you check Tense's belongings such as bank books and letters from Gogo when Tense is not home?"

"Well……………I………….."

"How do you find it out, Mr Leather?"

"Well……….."

"Do you cheat the Lecturers in Law course while Tense is studying that to fail Tense because you send people to the course as class-mates with Tense. Then after every examination the man Coo calls Tense. No matter what Tense tells Coo. Coo reports to Lecturers the false information and mislead the Lecturers to fail Tense. Is it correct?"

"Well……………..Well………………."

"Mr Leather, are you able to give a very good reasonable and plain answer to all the above questions I have just asked you?"

"…………………………"

After 3 or 4 years of all these incidents Leather is terribly ill and dies. His brothers and sisters still continue the fight for power, terror fight. Terri and Tense move away and never ever contact these means anymore from then on!

From this time onwards Terri and Tense both has a better, luckier and happier life. They go on smoothly and hoping Fairy does his power to retain happiness on both Terri and Tense!

These events happened in 2 episodes. Each time frame is 30 years! Good luck!

CHAPTER 17

In the court room,

"Mr Leather, as you said your second son Lance has got 4 to 5 houses to receive rental incomes. Is that correct?"

"Yes."

"Also Lance studies in country Cedar before migration. Is it correct?"

"Yes. Absolutely."

"You also, intentionally or accidentally, utter that Lance's study overseas has caused you a few hundreds of thousand dollars. Is that correct?"

"Certainly."

"What is the total amount, exactly?"

"May be 6 or 7 hundred thousand dollars!"

"May be?"

"Of course. May be!"

"Lance studied in country Cedar for 5 years but only has used 7 hundred thousand dollars. Are you lying to this Court, Mr Leather?"

"No, I am not!"

"To study 5 years but only spend less than 1 million dollars. Mr Leather do you personally believe in what you have just said?"

"Of course, what a silly question!"

"Take it 2 hundred thousand dollars a year because of 5-year study. Lance has to pay the rental expenses, to buy beverages, to buy textbooks, to have lunch on university campus or other restaurants and besides rental expenses Lance also has to pay the water and electricity payments. All these added up is 2 hundred thousand dollars. Mr Leather, are you kidding me?"

"No, I am not."

"You are not. Besides study Lance has got a motor vehicle to drive to campus and Lance goes on holidays every year. These added together is 2 hundred thousand dollars a year. Do you believe in that Mr Leather?"

"Of course."

"Besides study. Whenever going out to have lunch or dinner. Tense asks you for one more dish of food but refused. After one birthday dinner of Tense, Tense is still hungry but Lance is going out to have his own dinner or second dinner by himself because you already given money to Lance. Is that correct?"

"I can't remember the exact happenings."

"Once Tense asks you to give money to Tense for the simple food Tense has bought to eat before his evening class. This only costs around $150. But you show him your face. Is that true?"

"It is a lot of money. $150."

"Besides rental incomes Lance still asks you for cash. Each time is $500. Is that a lot of money, Mr Leather?"

"....................."

"While Lance is studying in country Aedoes, that is this country. You bought him a car but Tense asks you for a new car to Tense himself to drive to study you keep silence and not saying a word. Is that correct?

"Why didn't you reply, Mr Leather?

"It is because you are not fair to both of your biological sons! Is that correct, Mr Leather?"

"Tense has illness and cannot drive a car. Simple as that!"

"Why do you tell the neurologist not to prescribe medication to Tense while he is having problems with his dizziness?"

"He did not tell me."

"Tense is fighting against his illness. Then you have plenty of pretexts to impliedly show Tense not to study and not to work. Is it correct?

"Also once Lance drives Tense and yourself and your cousins to a doctor for Tense's cough. On return home Lance stops the car in the middle of the road. It really implies to Tense to figure your intentions that is to or not to give Tense a car. Same as before your migration. Also to demonstrate and certify your influences on Tense. Am I correct, Mr Leather?"

"Utterly rubbish!"

"What rubbish?"

"I comfort him not to be anxious and to relax every time he is having dizziness."

"Every time! It is because you are having your own problems at that time of year!"

"No, I have no problems."

"At that time you are a brain and heart disease patient suffering from enormous painful symptoms especially heart failures at that time of the year!"

"…………"

"It is you need the help of Tense to call a cab to go to hospital with you that you try and pretends to be good to Tense."

"No, I am not."

"You hate Tense so much. While you are diagnosed with cancer you call to Lance to ask him to come back from where he is working at that time. But it is because he refuses then your last resort is Tense to help you."

"I do not trust Tense."

"Tense has done everything to the best for you and you treat Terri and Tense like these? Are you a human or unconsciously hopeless animal?"

"…………………"

"Even a tiger does not eat its own cubs. Mr Leather!"

"……………"

"Terri does all housework from morning till late at night without grievances and was admitted to hospital. Meanwhile you wanted to divorce her. You even are happy to stay in harmony with the sisters who cause Terri to become a patient. On Tense behalf. Tense helps you every time you are having problems. Helps you every time you are in turmoils. But you always curse both of them as a crazy person to express your annoyance. Are you really a gentleman or a hypocrite, Mr Leather?"

"……………"

"Mr Leather, isn't that you always tell Tense not to marry the girls from another planet?"

"Yes, I do."

"What is the reason?"

"My wife Terri does not understand their language."

"Terri does not understand their language."

"Yeah, simple as that!"

"Why don't you say it is you do not understand their language?"

"Not this reason."

"It is you who does not understand their language you quietly oblige Tense not to marry these girls. By doing this you are able to communicate with your daughter-in-law. Then you are able to tell her to ask Tense to do this and to do that. At that moment Tense is still under your tightly control. You are still on the top of the world. Is it correct, Mr Leather?"

"Utterly rubbish!"

"Why do you tell Tense not to eat lamb chops served with tomato sauce and not to eat fish fingers also served with tomato sauce. Plus even not to drink coffee in the morning same as foreigners. Why?"

"It is because I am a diabetic patient. Tense will inherent diabetes with a more higher chance if he takes in too much sweet food such as tomato sauce."

"At this moment you are very good to Tense, aren't you?"

"I always am!"

"Not to eat too much at dinner while it is dining out. Plus not to have sweet food in case of catching diabetes. Also not to marry foreign girls. These are all for the good of Tense. Is that correct, Mr Leather?"

"Of course. Exactly!"

"Mr Leather, do you believe in what you have just told the court?"

"Of course I do."

"Then I ask Jury. Can the Jury figure what Mr Leather has told the court are all truths and trustworthy? Can we believe in his affidavit? Are we able to trust Mr Leather of what he has said and what he has done? Jury, one word in advance. Even God punishes Mr Leather by giving him the renal disease at the time he was born. It is crystal clear that it is absolutely the most important indication from God's message is that Mr Leather is really a hypocrite and a mean person who does evil dealings all the time. Or from his birth right to his death all are nasty handlings to harm and hurt other people even his biological son Tense and his married wife Terri for more than 40 years."

In the afternoon in court room the same day,

"Mr Leather, can you recall you always lose your temper to see Tense eats too much while Tense is working in your company LL?"

"Yes, of course."

"Why you are angry?"

"I never ever watch a person eats so much!"

"As stated before. You are not able to recall your wife Terri to eat 3 bowls of rice every meal during the time she is having baby Tense?"

"I am unable to recall."

"Really? At that time everyone realises it. Is it correct?"

"I can't remember."

"At later time while you are renovating your house. You invite the worker to lunch. Is it correct, Mr Leather?"

"Yes! Absolutely. The man asks for a place to discuss what to do on renovation."

"During the lunch all of you are eating. Right?"

"Yeah!"

"When the lunch is going to finish and everyone is having enough. You still call small dishes for Tense to eat. Correct?"

"Yes,"

"In that lunch the workman brings with him together with his girlfriend. Correct, Mr Leather?"

"Yeah!"

"After a few weeks you ask Tense quietly without anyone nearby and no one knows at that time. You ask Tense did he have enough? Is it true, Mr Leather?"

"Yes. I want to know he really did have enough."

"At that time you did not lose your temper?"

"................."

"You concern with Tense and want him good then?"

"................."

"You are happy to see him to eat plenty of food since?"

"After the death of your brother Little for more than 2 years. You once talk loudly in public and in front of Little's widow wife that other relatives go to dine with Little used to say the dishes are not as good as what you invite them to meals. Is it correct?"

"Yeah!"

"The food you ordered were or always are better than Little's. Right?"

"Yes. Of course!"

"Little's wife did not utter a single word?"

"No, she didn't."

"A few days later you intentionally say in front of Tense implying Little's wife is not so arrogant as she used to be in her earlier life. Correct?"

"Yeah! Absolutely."

"What you have said is a test or revenge to Little's wife?"

"I want to know is she really not so proud as before."

"You insult her in the first instance but it is only to find out what you are puzzling?"

"Yes."

"But the assault is already done."

"It is the only option."

"To insult somebody in order to find out the truth. The humiliation is the only means to implement?"

"No other choices!"

"In the first 2 years on your migration once your business partner telephoned you to argue on the company business. Then at the end of the telephone call he said, 'Do you know what I am talking about?' Then you said, 'Yes, I understand!'. Is this an insult, Mr Leather?"

"Absolutely!"

"Are you happy with this?"

"………………."

"Once you are talking to somebody. You mention that your business partner first asked all the details of what you were going to do in the coming days. Then he knew you were going to return to migrated country on New Year Eve. Then the business partner refused to do the ledgers in order that you had to delay your departure. Is it a fact, Mr Leather?"

"Yes, he did it."

"Were you annoy at that time, Mr Leather?"

"Yes, of course!"

"Is this an insult or dirty trick to delay your departure and then to negotiate with what he wanted to discuss?"

"Yes."

"He did it to you is an assault. But on the case of Tense all people did these types of tricks to Tense are not assaults but it is ONLY to test Tense is a good man or not. Is that what you want to tell the Court, Mr Leather?"

"It is true that Tense loses temper all the time."

"It is obviously to perform such tricks is good to Tense?"

"Yes."

"But why were you angry then?"

"................"

"To you is no good but to Tense is a perfect match. Is this correct, Mr Leather?"

"..................."

"Regarding to all these evidences cross-examined in this Court. I want the jury to decide is Mr Leather a good gentleman or an evil and inhuman hypocrite? What he does is to the benefits of himself only. Not to any single advantage to his wife or biological sons. He only pretends to be good to his siblings on pretexts that they were brought up by Leather and Leather knows their characters are good and deserved Leather's kind and respective concerns in return.

"I want the jury to tell this whole world what the hell is Leather doing. Is he fighting to establish his own dynasty to be run for centuries? Is he establishing his own empire that he is the real founder? Is he the man deserved to have all these reputations? Are all his methods used is under humanity axioms and within conscious design?

To sum up does this man. Mr Leather, deserved all the reputation of being a good and kind hearted gentleman or he is a cruel, inhuman and non-conscious animal but only put on human skin like a cunny wolf to cheat all other people in this World? And only does all non-conscience evil dealings in his life time.

"Jury, I want you to give a fair, unbiased and conscience verdict to this person, Mr Leather. Does he deserved to be called a gentleman? Otherwise is he a hypocrite? He always does anything that is for his own sake. He uses Terri and Tense to accomplish his lusts for power, reputations and personal influences. He tries every single method to go to his goal and never stops. Even he is very sick at that time he still figure means to hurt Tense in saying Tense is a patient and blames Terri by saying after their marriage Leather is not the beloved son of Laws. Also to return to unity with the 2 sisters who once cursed Leather himself.

Jury, please give an emotional and conscience verdict to this hypocrite. Meanwhile to uphold Terri and Tense's good housewife and good son's behaviour for the people of generations and generations to come to learn the best! Thank you!"

CHAPTER 18

In the court room,

"Mr Leather, is it not that you always say Tense does anything is bad, crazy and without logic?"

"Yes, he is."

"Does Tense listen to you to sit in the office room where the company is the partnership between your paternal uncle and yourself?"

"What for?"

"You want Tense to watch and observe what the people are doing in order to report to you as you have a quarrel with your uncle's son. Is it correct?"

"Yes, I said this before."

"Does Tense report to you exactly what he saw?"

"Yeah!"

"Did you satisfy of what he told you? Or did you have sufficient information after Tense disclosed all the details to you?"

"Yeah!"

"While, as stated before, you were together with your cousin having a court case with your uncle Less. Did Tense help you?"

"No, he did not."

"He did not?"

"No, he did not."

"Tense did not pray to Fairy or God to arrange this court case to go smoothly and then won the case?"

"No. It was all my merits as I was the only witness to give strong evidences to support the argument."

"Once you talked loudly on the telephone to your brother that your lawyer was extremely happy and said it was lucky because of that particular sudden directors' meeting. Is it correct?"

"Yes, it is."

"It is really luck as later you win the case?"

"Yes, of course!"

"It is not God's power to arrange this sudden meeting to let you win?"

"No, of course not!"

"It is all you have done that the case is won?"

"Of course."

"Mr Leather, do you have any conscience?"

"Of course I have."

"You once said some people do not have a red face when they are telling lies. But Mr Leather, on my behalf, you do not have a red face when you are lying and cheating other people. Simply you tried very hard when you were young to make your face is always dark as to conceal your dirty cunny behaviours and tricks."

"No, you are wrong."

"Where is the wrong?"

"............."

"Tense always help you and Terri always does the housework at home without going out to see the world simply because of your dictatorship. Now you are telling all the people in this world they are wrong. Mr Leather, take a cautious move after your death and then while you are talking and arguing and explaining to Fairy. To explain in detailed of what you have done in this life and to receive God's rewards or punishments. You even not go to monastery to say your prayers. Mr Leather!"

Later again in the court room,

"Mr Leather, as stated your opinion on Tense is he does not know how to manage matters logically and needs your surveillance. Is that correct?"

"Yes, simple as that!"

"And also Tense is very clever or too intelligent that he will commit crimes without other people's notices or even the police has no sufficient evidences to sue Tense. Is that correct?"

"Yeah!"

"As stated above Tense does everything to your best benefits. Tense listens to you and follow your advices. Such as Tense works in your company LL as a junior clerk not the son of the boss. Even the office boy's salary is more than what Tense has got. Is he doing right, Mr Leather?"

"He knows nothing. That's why he gets a lower salary!"

"He knows nothing!"

"Absolutely!"

"If he knows nothing. Why don't you teach him the business strategies but instead teach your office boy?"

"The office boy works hard and deserved I to teach him!"

"Tense does not work hard?"

"He is very lazy!"

"What lazy?"

"He cannot wake up early and becomes inert on every Saturday."

"Does he do something about it?"

"No, he doesn't!"

"Isn't that Tense drinks coffee on Saturday mornings at the first 6 months of his working period. It is to be energetic and lasts up to Saturday night?"

"I have no idea!"

"Do you watch him while he is drinking coffee?"

"   …   …   …   …   …   I   …   …   …   … do…………n………ah………….."

"What Tense and Terri do are to the best benefits of you. Now you are telling the court they are nasty people and Tense does not able to earn a profit for you. By this you silently consent the office boy to eye at Tense to humiliate Tense and you are very happy in doing these. Am I correct, Mr Leather?"

"Rubbish!"

"You use the pretext that Tense is too clever to do crimes and walk free from the court. Then Tense needs your surveillance. Is it correct, Mr Leather?"

"Of course."

"But do you understand, again you are a follower of Fairy. Does a Fairy or even God's beloved son Jesus Christ. When they come to earth to preach, do they commit crimes or do they need to be checked up every now and then, Mr Leather?"

"Well…………it …………..is………..ah…………"

"Mr Leather, can you explain to the court that what you have done as compared to what Terri and Tense have done. The results are all to your good meanwhile both Terri and Tense are nasty. Is it correct?"

"Absolutely true!"

"What good things you have done?"

"…………………….."

"To humiliate the office boy after you found out he is not loyal to you. To humiliate Tense once he is a patient. To humiliate the neurologist while you have no one to express your anger. You try to insult the office boy secretly without the notice of Tense. Is this your revenge to Cha's dishonesty to you and humiliations to all those people you are able to condemn?

To uphold and support your cousin in the court case against Less is good simply Less does all things are bad. In that case why you praised Less as a skilful businessman who can manage many storms and chaos on the commercial areas before your cousin asks for your help? Why don't you sue Less by yourself?"

"Simply I have no money."

"You have no money and then you have to support Less and follow what he does even nasty things but only later to quarrel with him on illegal issues that you spelt out whenever you mention these illegal affairs or when complaining to other people while you are cursing Less for his wrong doings which at that time you are on the side of your cousin who is a billionaire who wants to sue Less. Is it the right thing to do, Mr Leather?"

"I have no choice!"

"No choice and you have to support Less?"

"What can I do?"

"You do not go out to work instead and do not have your own business to earn money to establish your business empire. Whenever you have cash earned from your own business then you can sue Less simply he eats the shares of Laws in the company. Instead you curse Less and this is the only option?"

"I don't have a chance, simple as that!"

"Why do you have no money? Your cousin is also doing the same business but he has a lot of money to sue Less meanwhile you have not. Does it make sense, Mr Leather?"

"Laws does not leave money to me!"

"While you are working in the family business. You have your salary of $600 every month. After 10 months of marriage you do not have money to pay the specialist and the hospital fees. Where has the money gone?

Also after your father's death you were given 110 shares of the company. At that time episode it was less than 20 years before you and your brothers sold the company shares to your cousin Mr Lang. The time you sold the shares is that you only sold 50 shares. Where are the other 60 shares gone? Mr Leather?"

"I need to socialise with the clients and my friends. It's simple!"

"Your brothers are keeping their own shares the same number as they were given after Laws's death. Your brother also has a family to support and children to be raised up. They are able to retain the shares and you are in the same position but you can't. Your brother Letton goes for holidays with his whole family every year. Letton is also a worker in a company and you are presumed as the boss. Why did you spend so much, Mr Leather? Are these all should be expended as a way of doing business, Mr Leather?

"To socialise and to use up all the salary and to leave behind Terri and Tense at home while you have good dishes and delicious food on your own. This is business?"

"This is what a businessman doing! What's wrong with it?"

"To do business only to let Terri becomes a patient and to divorce Terri and goes back to harmony with your 2 sisters Lie and Lin. While these are the right things to do. Is that right, Mr Leather?"

"I can marry any girls as my wife but I can't let my siblings to resurrect like Jesus Christ, can I?"

"After the death of your father Laws. It should be the most favourite person to talk to and to discuss any matter and that person should be and ought to be your wife Terri. But now you are saying you can divorce and re-marry. Do you have your conscience or can you promise to Fairy and God what you have done are all correct without a single error and they are extremely perfect?"

"……………I……………well…………"

"The court is waiting for your answer, Mr Leather!"

"……………………….."

"Mr Leather, as all you have said. Are you able to promise to Fairy and God all you have done are correct?"

"If I have done anything wrong. I will die!"

At this time Leather is already under the care of a renal specialist. Before this event around 10 or 12 months earlier Leather is happily going on holidays for 3 months whenever he is happy. During the vacation Leather goes out to eat every day. Every morning Leather eats an egg as served by the fast food restaurant for totally 3 months.

After this holidays Leather comes back home and goes for blood test. The test indicates his kidney is going even worse. The renal function is starting to deteriorate faster than expected. After around 2 years later Leather dies on renal failure.

Again in the court room,

"Mr Leather, as you have said you send your followers to dog Tense wherever he goes. Is it right?"

"No, I haven't!"

"You haven't! Now you haven't!"

"Of course not."

"But how do you know what Tense is doing outside?"

"Tense tells me."

"He tells you?"

"Yeah, he tells me!"

"Does Tense always tell you not to disclose whatsoever Tense does to other people. This is to evade the chances that nasty people have a chance to harm Tense or even kill Tense. Is that correct?"

"No, he hasn't told me that!"

"No?"

"No."

"You do not send people to follow Tense. You have no idea what Tense is doing outside the home area. How do you keep an eye on him as you stated to the court just a few hours ago?"

"………………"

"You do not tell other people of what Tense has done. Your followers can inform you of Tense is already applied a part time job outside. Are you able to explain to the court, Mr Leather?"

"I only realised when Tense is going to attend his part time job on the morning after he received the telephone call."

"Simple as that?"

"Yeah! Simple as that!"

"Why do you have lunch with Mr Fan on that very afternoon?"

"It is coincident."

"Really?"

"Yes for sure!"

"After that day (Sunday) you stay home and waiting for the telephone call from the part time job company to call Tense. On this conversation you pretend to be talking to criminal offenders. Is that correct?"

"He called my home number."

"What did you say then?"

"He said go to start your work. Then I said, 'Start what work?'!"

"Then?"

"He hangs up."

"Only these?"

"Yes for sure!"

"How do you get the information that Tense has applied the part time job? Again how can you introduce the girl friends to Tense while Tense is outside of the office room?"

"Tense tells me what he is doing outside."

"He tells you?"

"Yeah!"

"What does he tell you?"

"He tells me he is learning Martial Arts somewhere close to Happy Point Bay."

"The point is how can you introduce a girl to Tense whenever Tense only tells you he is learning Martial Arts but you can introduce girl friends to Tense?"

"He knows the girl then tells me afterwards!"

"Really?"

"Yeah!"

"How do you let the girl you are going to introduce to Tense to let the girl also learning Martial Arts in the same class as Tense?"

"………………"

"Do you tell other people all the things Tense does?"

"No, I don't."

"How do all these people know what Tense is doing at the time?"

"……………"

"Look at the Martial Arts class. No one knows Tense is attending the class. On the contrary, you are able to introduce a girl to Tense in that very same class to learn Martial Arts with Tense. How does the girl get there, Mr Leather?"

"I do not know the girl. But the girl tells me afterwards. I think!"

"How does the girl know you, Mr Leather?"

"…………………"

"You always imply to Tense simply to say anything he does Tense has to tell you. Is that correct?"

"He tells me himself."

"You just said he told you. After Tense has told you about his affairs. Do you tell other people?"

"No, I do not!"

"You always imply to Tense that you are worry about Tense simply he is more cleverer than other people. By this he is able to commit crimes without other people's notices. How can you keep your surveillances, Mr Leather?"

"........................."

"Tense tells you all Tense has known and you betray Tense to say all these things that Tense has told you to outsiders to let people to harm Tense. Whenever Tense is in trouble you can stand up as a gentleman to help Tense. But instead it is you who create all of these chaos. Is that right, Mr Leather?"

"..................."

"Mr Leather, as you told the court earlier you help to wash the floor of your residence with Terri. Is that right?"

"Yeah! Absolutely!"

"Why you do not do the job afterwards?"

"Tense says he replaces my position."

"Why Tense says this?"

"I have no idea!"

"Tense as stated you told the court earlier before he sees you are having neck troubles and washing floor is hard and difficult job. That's why Tense replaces you, is that right Mr Leather?"

"I think so!"

"Besides it is a hard work consumed job. Is there any other reasons behind all these of what you have told this Law Court, Mr Leather?"

"No, I don't think so. Honestly!"

"What laundry powder you use to wash the floor?"

"It is Pet's powder, I think!"

"It is a very old style of laundry cleaning powder. Any other washing fluids, Mr Leather?"

"Also dish washing liquids."

"These are all old fashioned and out of date commodities to be consumed nowadays."

"It is what Terri told Tense to buy from supermarket."

"You say nothing?"

"I don't know what to use to wash the floor."

"You don't know?"

"I am a businessman. I only know how to do business. Nothing else!"

"At that time there are already many new products for consumption. You know nothing about all these cleaning products. Mr Leather?"

"I have not a single clue!"

"Not a single hint!"

"Not a single tip!"

"You always watch television, don't you?"

"Yes, I watch TV."

"You don't know anything about the new washing products?"

"………Well…………I………….think………."

"There are no ads on these new cleaning products?"

"………..I…………"

"How long does it take for Terri to wash and clean the house every time?"

"It makes her to work for a whole day."

"Where are you then?"

"I go out."

"Where?"

"I bring Tense to the Medical Doctor and then have lunch in restaurants."

"Meanwhile Terri is staying home to work?"

"Yeah! What's the problem?"

"You always say that all your family members are told to work. You go out for lunch. Your sister stays at home after examinations and not to look for a job but your comment is that she is a good girl under any circumstances. Simply they are your siblings. While other people's siblings especially Terri's are no good. Are you able to explain to this court what are the reasons behind your dogmatic explanations, Mr Leather?"

"……………………………………….."

"The court is waiting for your answer, Mr Leather!"

"………………….."

"The court is waiting for your answer, Mr Hypocrite!"

"…………………………….."

"Again Mr Leather are you able to recall the scenario that one night around 8pm your sister-in-law called Tense to come out to have dinner?"

"What was that?"

"At the restaurant there were other people eating food there. Your sister-in-law served Tense to sit down and ordered a dish."

"What then?"

"The restaurant is a high-class restaurant. While Tense was there you only gambled at a table without take a look at Tense."

"Then?"

"Then after Tense had dinner your sister-in-law told Tense to leave."

"What followed?"

"At that night you did not utter a single word to Tense. Is that correct, Mr Leather?"

"What's the problem?"

"Isn't that you showed your face to Tense, Mr Leather?"

"I was playing cards!"

"After that night did Tense say any good words in front of you, Mr Leather?"

"No, he didn't."

"Did Tense say anything that you are great and intelligent?"

"No, he didn't."

"Did Tense say something that you are honest, humble and reliable, Mr Leather?"

"No, he didn't."

"Is that you want Tense to say all these words to you. Then Tense shows himself as lusts for power and money. Such that you can use this advantage to control Tense to accomplish your ugly and cunny goals as a real gentleman in front of other people. Is that correct, Mr Leather?"

"No, it isn't."

"Then why did you not talk to Tense on that night?"

"I was playing cards."

"Why did you show your face to Tense, Mr Leather?"

"No, I did not."

"You always accuse your uncle Less shows his face to people. What you are doing is exactly the same as Less. Is that right, Mr Leather?"

"No, it is wrong."

"Why didn't you talk nor even took a look at Tense on that night?"

"……………….."

"Why didn't you talk nor took a look at Tense on that night, Mr Leather?"

"………………………………….."

"Mr Leather, do you remember you visit your maternal uncle in nursery home while you are returning to home town after migration?"

"Yes, I do!"

"Why you visit your maternal uncle?"

"He cannot walk and needs other people such as nurses or healthcare practitioners to help his daily routines."

"Such as ……..?"

"Such as help him to eat his meals everyday as he cannot move his fingers and feet properly."

"Only these?"

"Yes, only these!"

"Mr Leather, regarding what Tense told the court. Terri told Tense that at the time you are working in your family business. Once you visit your client retailer shop and fortunately you meet your maternal uncle. As soon as you see your uncle. You immediately turn around and go back home. Is it correct?"

"I can't recall."

"When you are home. You shout loudly for more than 4 times that you saw your uncle and you hurry home and not to talk to your uncle. Is it correct, Mr Leather?"

"I don't think so!"

"While your maternal uncle is in nursery home. You do not pay any visit to him. It is only Tense asks about uncle's health status then you start your visit every time you are back in your home town. Is it correct?"

"Does Tense say all these?"

"Of course, he does."

"These are all rubbish!"

"Rubbish?"

"Tense is a patient. What he says are not trustworthy!"

"Not to be trusted by anybody?"

"No, absolutely no!"

"At your later life every time you go back to your home town. Your maternal uncle's son, that is your relative always invite you to lunch. Is that true, Mr Leather?"

"Yes, it is correct. What's the problem?"

"At that time do you mention anything about the occasion you ignored your uncle?"

"No, I don't"

"Why?"

"It is the dispute between my father and my uncle. I have no obligation to say or comment on their dispute. Honestly, both are now dead. It is not to say better to mention the dispute to their offspring."

"At that time you are happy to be a good friend with your relative then?"

"Yes, why not?"

"Another matter Mr Leather you always tell your siblings and any person who talk to you. You inform them you are from the background of doing business. Thus, you are skilful in commercial tactics and the tricks merchants always implement to cheat other people. Do I say anything wrong?"

"No, you are correct!"

"Then your relative is able to accept his father's business and altering to other fashion business and financial dealings with other new clients?"

"Yes, he is good!"

"Why you can't, then?"

"He is smart, not me to be honest! Ha, ha ...."

"At that time he is your good relative and no or not to have any dispute. Correct, Mr Leather?"

"....................."

"Mr Leather, why you need your another uncle called you to have partnership with him as mentioned earlier. Meanwhile you cannot go out to set up your own business after your father's death?"

"I have no money, frankly!"

"You are the son of the boss and you don't have any cash?"

"My father and uncle insist to control the economic conditions of the descendants. They won't allow children to take money from the business unless we ask them or tell them in detail why we need money."

"Simple as that?"

"It is feudalism, isn't it, Mr Barrister?"

"But your relative is able to take money out from his father's business?"

"I have no idea what is going on there. I can't comment on this, sorry!"

"Another question Mr Leather, once you quarrelled with your mother-in-law, that is Terri's mother over the phone. You accuse her son, that is the billionaire Tom, not to go to your brother's funeral. Do I say anything wrong?"

"Tom is no conscience!"

"What do you mean?"

"My brother helped Tom to buy profitable businesses at a terribly cheap price. But he does not go."

"You told your mother-in-law this and say Tom is not doing what he should do. Is it right, Mr Leather?"

"Of course!"

"From Tense's affidavit Tense recalls you once told your sisters when your brother who was working in Tom's office. That is the brother who helped Tom to buy the businesses. When your brother resigned Tom gave him $20,000 as compensation or redundancy. You even said it is because of Tom' relation with you. Therefore, Tom gave this extra amount to your brother. Is it correct?"

"................."

"You quarrelled with your mother-in-law on the phone saying Tom is no good. What is your position then, Mr Leather?"

"My position is to help my siblings to have a better life!"

"Why don't you mention anything about your power struggle with your siblings. Mr Leather?"

"We have no arguments!"

"Really?"

"Of course!"

"Mr Leather after all these cross-examinations. I have confidence to tell the court and jury that whatsoever you do good things. You are going to tell everybody. All the ugly things you do you will never ever utter a single word on this. Am I wrong?"

"Of course you are incorrect!"

"Where am I incorrect?"

"I am a good gentleman. All people know this!"

"You are a good gentleman?"

"Of course, what a silly question?"

"Let's say it this way. You are the opposite side of a good gentleman. Okay?"

"No!"

"Why then?"

"........................"

Both Terri and Tense hope to have a better future after all these happenings. May Fairy have mercy on Terri and Tense! Hopefully! Still a wish! May be all will change to a better status! Why not?

Printed in the United States
By Bookmasters